Rolo Diez, born in Argentina
for two years during the r.
forced into exile. He now lives in Mexico City, where
he works as a novelist, screenwriter and journalist. A
number of his novels have been published in Spain,
France and Germany. Rolo Diez was awarded the
Hammett prize for best crime novel in Spanish in
1985, and won the Umbriel Prize at the Semana Negra
festival of crime fiction in Spain in 2003. This is the
first time he has been published in English.

TEQUILA BLUE

Rolo Diez

Translated from the Spanish by Nick Caistor

BITTER LEMON PRESS
LONDON

BITTER LEMON PRESS

First published in the United Kingdom in 2004 by
Bitter Lemon Press, 37 Arundel Gardens, London W11 2LW

www.bitterlemonpress.com

First published in Spanish as *Mato y Voy* by
Ediciones B, Mexico City, 1992

Bitter Lemon Press gratefully acknowledges the financial assistance
of the Arts Council of England

© Rolo Diez, 1992
English translation © Nick Caistor, 2004

A CIP record for this book is available from the British Library

ISBN 1–904738–04–4

Typeset by RefineCatch Limited, Broad Street, Bungay, Suffolk
Printed and bound in Great Britain by
Bookmarque Ltd, Croydon, Surrey

For Myriam

Chapter one

Snow White looks eighteen going on fifteen, with her short skirt and plaits, breasts like apples and 110 pounds of a mixture of innocence and sensuality all wrapped in tissue paper. There are only four, not seven dwarfs, and they are not real dwarfs, just very short men. Half-hidden behind false white beards, their faces are vicious and disturbing. The opening scene shows them having a meal in a clearing in a wood. One of the dwarfs is serving wine. He offers it to Snow White but switches the bottle without her realizing it. The four freaks wink and make obscene gestures to one other. They watch lasciviously as the woman-child sips from her glass. As she finishes her drink, Snow White falls into what appears to be a catatonic trance. The dwarfs pull a mattress out from under the table. They lay Snow White down on it and start undressing her.

Chapter two

Lourdes woke me at eight with a beer and a sour look that I had no intention of responding to. I twisted and turned in the bed until I was more or less upright and could take the first swig.

"I went to bed at four," I told her. "This beer is warm. I don't want it frozen, but it should be cold. I've told you a thousand times."

Lourdes is the only person in the world who can launch into four different topics at once:

"You told me you were leaving at eight; we haven't paid the kids' school fees; there's nothing to eat; why do you have a family if you can't be bothered to look after them?"

Lourdes is thin, the nervous type, her beauty ruined by her irritation. I contemplated a reply, but it sank without trace in my desire to go on sleeping.

"Put the beer in the freezer and call me again in fifteen minutes."

Lourdes walked off complaining, but I wasn't even listening any more. Cops like me can sleep standing up, when we're on duty, covering some guy whose footsteps are bound to wake us up.

An hour later I was out of the house. The sun

hurt my eyes, and the fumes from Avenida Revolucion clawed at my nose and throat.

I stopped off at a taco bar and had a quick breakfast. A soup with bread and lots of chilli in it – the perfect indigenous remedy to improve the way a hung-over guy sees the world, the human condition, and Mondays, to help persuade him he has to go to the office – then chopped steak and several coffees. The bar owner, Luis, wanted to know the price on .38 revolvers and 9mm pistols.

"I've got someone interested in buying," he said with a wink. "I could order five or six, if there's something in it for me."

"I'll look into it," I told him. "I'll tell you tomorrow."

I was thinking of talking to Amaya, who can get rods cheap. If each of us made a hundred thousand on each gun, that would mean half a million for us and we could still sell them at a reasonable price. Not business for its own sake, but to fight the debts that insisted on piling up at the end of every month.

Red was not at the money exchange: he had a business breakfast. And the envelope for my boss wasn't there either. That scumbag Red: the Commander wasn't going to be pleased at having to wait. I'd left Red thirty thousand dollars on his behalf, first-class Colombian stuff that even the White House would accept. And he was supposed to pay up today. He knew that, but here he was, playing games with cops . . . as if we couldn't screw his business completely if we felt like it.

"What time is he coming?" I asked.

"He won't be long," his secretary said.

A nymphette, a looker. Hot stuff, but not as hot as she thought she was.

Her office was all glass, wall-to-wall carpet, paintings and diplomas. I undid my jacket. I was sitting so that little miss pretty couldn't see the grease stain on my trousers. I used to be able to sit with my jacket buttoned, but these days my stomach seems determined to put on a display of forty years of tacos and beer.

"Has he been in touch?" I said, putting on my stern policeman look. I know these dames. If you so much as let on you've noticed their attractions, there's no end to their little games of seduction. Not because a tart like her gives a damn about someone like me, but simply because it's their way of showing their power. The only power they've got: flesh and their shiny veneer.

"No," with a flutter of rings and bangles. "But he usually comes in about now."

"I need to talk to him urgently," I said, handing her my card. "Please tell him to call me as soon as he gets here."

"Yes, Mr Hernandez," she said, looking at the card.

I buttoned my jacket and stood up. I leaned over to shake hands, and found myself staring down a plunging neckline. She saw my look and smiled.

*

When I got to the office they were serving coffee. The Commander was having breakfast in the Sheraton with a judge and a member of Congress. Convinced that public relations are all about having a full stomach and a full diary, the boss doesn't stint on breakfast. He devotes his mornings to other people's careers and tries to choose the right people.

Maribel brought me coffee. She stroked my hand and asked for my office contribution: fifty thousand pesos.

"You owe the last two payments," she said, her voice as sweet and fake as her expression.

Maribel is as hot as her native Veracruz, and is battling against time. Her hair is dyed and teased at the salon. She has good legs, adolescent children she prefers to keep hidden, a baker husband, and the soul of a whore. Just because she's the boss's secretary she thinks she can intimidate and lay – or at least try to lay – all the males in the office. I think of her every time I hear a feminist banging on about the sexual harassment of women in the workplace.

Maribel put on her best tropical smile and slid out the tip of her tongue: a promise of fellatio that set my stomach tingling.

All I had in my pockets was a fifty-peso bill. All I had to face a long day, feed myself, and find another ten of the same to calm Lourdes's nerves. Not to mention Gloria: I haven't been to her place in four days, and although she's patient enough and understands how difficult things can be, she's got kids and all the rest to take care of just like in any family. If I hadn't forbidden it, she'd be on the phone to me right now.

Maribel's knees closed in on mine. Laura and the cleaning woman exchanged knowing smiles. I didn't move.

"Wait till tomorrow, I'll pay you then," I said.

"Poor you! You've got so many problems." When they come over all tender, tarantulas must look exactly as she did at that moment. "How about going out for a drink, then you can tell me all about it?"

"The boss might arrive," I said half-heartedly.

"We've got an hour," whispered Maribel, with all the naturalness of someone who behaves in a Mexican police office as if she were Marlene Dietrich in a Cairo cabaret. She accompanied her words with increased pressure of her knees against my left leg, which I had to push against the floor to steady myself.

Seeing that the whole office was having fun at my expense, and considering a gentleman should never disappoint a lady, especially if he doesn't want to be thought of as a queer, I decided it would be less costly to have an early-morning fuck in a hotel at her expense than have to give her all I had left to pay my contribution.

In the elevator Maribel gave me a playful lipsticky bite that I returned as best I could.

"Beast!" she groaned with satisfaction.

"Don't leave any marks!" I told her, imagining Lourdes's face twisted with jealousy, and her mania for examining my neck and back for signs of someone else's nails and teeth. Lourdes is a self-taught forensic expert, and I'm always the man in the dock. We've had real arguments over it, and it's incredible how she spots these things!

On the way to the hotel in my hostess's Caribe, I was suddenly worried my trouser tool might not be up to it, or might be up to it then duck out half-way through the performance, or I might come too soon, as occasionally happens, especially when I have to examine a new body that's poring over mine. And even though Maribel was no stranger, I was worried about my size. I'm forty years old and see myself in the shower every day. Yet I'm still not sure whether I'm hung like a horse and make every woman swoon, as I sometimes think, or if what I've got is nothing more than the tiniest shrivelled up little bean in the world, not big enough to satisfy a cat on a diet.

At the hotel I ordered a rum and mineral water for my nerves and my thirst, both of which are par for the course in rooms like this. Exciting sounds were coming from the room next door, as if an Aztec virgin were being sacrificed on an altar. Interestingly, our bed was against the same wall: either a hippie or a communist idea that struck me as very clever. I soon changed my mind when it was obvious Maribel's interest in my charms was transferred to the wall. She stuck to it like a limpet. Naked and as wrinkled as an accordion, I lit a cigarette. Groans and sighs accompanied me all the way to the bathroom, where I pissed with

7

difficulty and found a glass. My professional training led me to take it back into the bedroom, place the top against the noisiest part of the wall and gesture for Maribel to come over and press her ear to it. Judging by the growing signs of ecstasy on her face, this had the desired effect. After I'd finished my cigarette, and given that a naked man can't stand around with his hands in his pockets, I started to undress her. Far from the pressures of offices and marriages, she let me get on with it. I undid her blouse and her bra, nibbling at her neck as I did so. I was still holding the glass in one hand while with the other I stroked her underarms, aroused her nipples with my fingers, bit her shoulder blades, licked her spinal column and at the same time encouraged her clothes on their slow journey to the floor. I lifted her skirt over her head. I took my time at her waist, filled both hands with her buttocks then started to take down her undies. Maribel was groaning, purring, her ear still pressed to the glass. I slid her pants down the narrow part of her legs. Maribel lifted one red shoe and freed herself. That was the moment I realized the gods were rewarding me for being such an excellent cop: I was going to make love to a woman whose head was buried in her skirt; I was going to fornicate with a woman who was listening to another couple fornicating; I was about to fuck a woman who still had her stockings and high-heeled shoes on. Three sexual fantasies in a single fuck! My prick flew up like an acrobat. I couldn't remember ever having seen it so big and strong. I pushed it between her buttocks and set about taking her from behind. Maribel turned towards me, smiled rapturously and whispered:

"My back's incredibly itchy. You couldn't scratch it for me, could you, love?"

For the next seven minutes I scratched her back, convinced no power on earth could ever make me erect again.

Afterwards, when we got round to sighing and then to silence after the sighs, she wanted the whole works. Disaster. I only just managed to get her to pay for the hotel and drinks. I'd been thinking of touching her for a loan, but it hardly seemed the right moment.

*

Back at the office, the boss had one of his "we're going to get a few things straight" faces on. To rub it in, as usual, he kept on about what time it was and how I had gone off with his secretary. He wasn't that bothered – in fact he was probably grateful, because if someone else didn't do it, he would have to – but he was the boss, and had to show who was in charge. Then he quickly turned to what really interested him. No news from Red. Purple veins stood out in the bags round his eyes as he stared at me in a way I was well accustomed to: I was to blame for everything. And even though my role was simply as a go-between who had to appear and collect the money from someone who wasn't there, we were talking about thirty thousand dollars, so there was no way the Commander was going to be reasonable about it.

"I'll call him right now," I said, playing the part of Officer Hernandez to perfection. "And he'd better have the money in his hand, or else!"

The boss's wrinkles lost some of their creases. He began to lecture me on the need to take strict measures against traffickers whose only thought was to get all the dollars they could out of the country, who thought nothing of Mexico because money was the only homeland they believed in. He went on to describe Red himself, who, to judge by the thoughts he expressed, was so unworthy and unreliable he could not understand why he had ever entrusted any dollars to him.

With his exhortation to behave with all the firmness characteristic of the DO still ringing in my ears, I left the boss's office. "Get a move on with that, because a gringo's been killed in a row between queers, and I want you to be in charge of the case" were the last words I heard.

*

It was usually a case with a gringo or involving people who could not be tainted with even the slightest whiff of suspicion, the kind of thing that could not be left to illiterate uniformed cops.

That's what we in the DO are here for, to operate with our sharp surgeon's knife on the gangrenous social body, to give precision treatment to events which, left to inexpert hands, might produce negative, even uncontrollable results.

And even though our critics – there are always critics, because there's more envy in this country than there are husbands whose wives have been fucking around – say our aims were drawn up by the comic Cantinflas, we know what we're worth.

When the Directorate of Operations was set up, the old guard was up in arms. "All operations are secret. Only senators and undersecretaries could think of associating them with publicity."

In private they said much harsher things.

Eighteen years on, they still think we're a bunch of pseudo-intellectual politicos on the make, and even though we have a smaller budget than any other department, none of the cops can forgive us for being able to write our own names.

As I left the office, Maribel did not even deign to look at me.

*

I called Lourdes from a payphone, and I have to say that she had only herself to blame for her foul mood. To calm her down, I told her I had the money in my pocket, and a desk groaning under piles of work; I suggested she get some things on credit from the store and promised I'd settle everything that evening. She asked me no less than three times if I really had the money, if I wasn't just trying to pull the wool over her eyes, and if this wasn't simply another of my stories. That woman's ability to doubt everything defies belief. I reassured her as best I could, then I got angry and hung up.

I wanted to hear more pleasant sounds, so I rang Gloria. No sooner did she hear my voice than the tears started. She accused me of being cruel, of abandoning her, of starving her children to death. Although I know she can be a bit over the top, I was annoyed that she seemed to be blaming me for everything too. I can remember a time when she made do with nothing, always had a smile for me and was a quiet oasis where I could rest whenever my wife was displaying her talents as a harpy. Though they had never met, in five years Gloria had become so similar to Lourdes they were like sisters. I swore I'd call in at her apartment that evening and promised to take money and presents for the kids.

Red was still not in his office. The nymphette told me in a singsong voice: "Doctor Rosenthal has flown to Guanajuato, but he left a message for you: he's very sorry and asks you to forgive the delay. He's got your money, and he'll settle everything first thing tomorrow."

Chapter three

Up in the sky above me I can see clouds and crows sailing past. Bound hand and foot to a sacrificial altar on the platform of a low pyramid, I watch as a priest offers me extreme unction in a language I do not understand. The priest is wearing a dagger at his waist; a frothing green mist rises from the goblet in his hands. It must be an acid or poison that will dissolve my flesh like wax.

"This is the punishment for disbelievers," the priest tells me. "This is what you get for voting for Cuauhtemoc Cardenas."

He tips the goblet. As the liquid falls onto my face, its icy needles empty out my eyes then fill the sockets, and the frozen fire slowly penetrates my brain.

The urge to stay alive forced me upright in bed, screaming and waving my arms in the air. I saw Lourdes's mocking, angry face and sat motionless while she finished pouring the contents of the beer bottle over my head.

Then Lourdes spoke, and her words made no more sense than the priest's litany.

"I'm tired of being your mother, Carlos!" she said. "I'm tired of your betraying me with every woman you meet! I've had it up to here and

13

beyond with all your lies! I'm sick and tired of how useless you are, how you can't even support your own family! I'm leaving you right now. As soon as I can, I'll take the children. And do me a favour – don't say a word. Don't even think of trying to explain anything."

"Hang on a minute!" Soaked and annoyed, uncertain whether to slap her or try to talk, I jumped out of bed.

Lourdes raised the bottle over her head.

"Come any closer and I'll crush your balls!" she threatened.

I collapsed onto a chair. I let my wife walk out on me without lifting a finger. I understood that her irrationality and egotism had leaped over all the barriers of self-censorship and shame and taken over every aspect of her character.

I went to the bookshelves – fifteen hundred works, some of them classics inherited from my father, others erotic novels or thrillers, or textbooks from my school days, penal codes and other legal volumes – took down *Philosophy in the Boudoir* by the Marquis de Sade. I pretended to be enjoying reading it until Lourdes slammed the door behind her.

I lit a cigarette and got another beer from the fridge. I walked round the flat drinking and smoking. Lourdes had not even bothered to make the kids' beds while they were at school. On the dining-room table I found a sealed envelope for the children, marked "For Carlos and Araceli". God knows what she could have to say as she abandoned them. I considered steaming the letter open but in the end couldn't be bothered. I had a shower, then discovered that the bath towel was missing. I was indignant that she could have been so selfish as to take it. I was forced to wipe myself dry using dirty clothes from the basket. I had a shave and put on my brown suit, the only one of my three outfits still relatively decent. Only the previous day I had been thinking of getting Lourdes to take my grey one to the dry-cleaner's. In my stomach, a third-world protest demonstration was starting up to demand something more substantial than tar and barley juice. A thorough investigation of fridge and larder produced only disheartening results. In my house everything, absolutely everything, gets eaten, in unbelievable amounts. They say that rats are the living beings capable of eating the widest variety of substances. I reckon an objective comparison between rats and my family could lead to a change of opinion. I found two half-rotten bananas, a bit of cheese so old it was fit only for worms and cockroaches, a carton of milk I decided to keep for my children (they're growing so they need it more than me, besides which I hate the stuff), a few dried-out frozen tortillas and a bottle of *chipotle* chilli sauce. Fortunately, there were some beers. I always keep one or two handy, so that I can have some cold whenever I feel like it. I have to take care of this myself, seeing how little I can count on Lourdes for anything that might concern me.

I decided to eat some tacos near the office.

Before leaving the flat I called the money exchange, where a male voice told me Doctor Rosenthal was away on a trip and they had no idea when he would be back. I put on my tough voice: "This is Officer Carlos Hernandez, and I need to speak to Rosenthal urgently, so please give me his address and personal telephone number." The person at the other end was obviously worried and answered: "One moment please", then left me hanging on for ten minutes. Eventually another man came on the line, introducing himself as Perez Blanco, the firm's accountant. I pictured him as someone who wore a well-pressed grey suit, had thinning, neatly brushed hair, and used tortoiseshell glasses. A dumb-looking asshole, one of those unbearable pedants who think they have the right to say and do whatever they like provided they are unctuous and polite with it. He began by saying he was at my service for anything concerning the business. I pressed him for Red's address and phone number. As calm as could be, Perez Blanco said he was very sorry but he did not have Doctor Rosenthal's address, as he had recently moved, to San Angel, he believed. He added that he would be delighted to give me the phone number, but that unfortunately he did not have it to hand. Besides which, he understood that Doctor Rosenthal's telephone was out of order and had not yet been repaired.

"This is the police," I explained. "I'll give you one minute to get the number and give it to me."

"Yes. One moment."

I could hear the accountant Perez Blanco breathing heavily. Twenty seconds later, I was dialling Red's number. A velvety voice came on the line to tell me: "The number you have dialled is out of service; we regret any inconvenience this may cause you." I suggested something the velvety lips could do for me that would be sure to end all my inconveniences, then hung up.

I called the money exchange once more. I said who I was and asked to speak to Rosenthal's secretary. The same male voice from my previous call informed me that as of the day before Miss Esparza no longer worked for them. I asked to speak to Perez Blanco again and was told: "He's just gone out." I didn't have to pretend to be angry when I asked whether Rosenthal himself still worked for them, and the voice at the other end – a spineless, pathetic sort, I surmised – was not pretending either when he expressed concern that no, Doctor Rosenthal was no longer with them, although there were still some loose ends for him to tie up. In fact, they were expecting him to arrive, or at least to hear from him, during the course of the day. I asked for his name – "Teodor-GomezAtYourService" – so I barked "Tell him to phone me today without fail."

*

En route to the office I was furious. I was counting on that money for Gloria's expenses. I was a bit behind in looking after her, and although she never goes short Gloria likes to moan over nothing. From her voice on the phone and some of the things she had said to me, I could tell she was on the verge of an attack of nerves.

It was twenty-five past ten, and I had an appointment with the gringo's wife at half past. Just time to call in on Luis and sort out the sale of the guns.

For half a mile I was stuck behind a stupid old bat who shouldn't even have been in charge of a supermarket trolley. I had to switch my siren on and run into her bumpers a couple of times for her to get out of the way. As I sped past she looked over at me in terror. I gave her the middle finger in a classic suggestion she should go fuck her ancestors.

"The deal's done, Luis," I told him when I finally got to the bar. "The parabellums are eight hundred dollars. I'll let you have them for seven hundred, so you'll make a hundred on each. I'll bring them tomorrow. But I need a bit of an advance to buy them."

Luis looked at me suspiciously.

"That's way over, Carlos," he said. "I've been offered some long-barrelled .38s for four hundred. You'll have to drop the price."

I struggled with the sausage and potatoes lying listlessly on my plate, took a good swig of coffee and then started slowly in on my chocolate flan.

"Six bullets, short range, no precision: that's a revolver for you. Plus you've no idea where they've come from. And God forbid, but if anyone is caught some day with one of them in his hand,

18

you can bet your boots even the most stupid cop will discover it was the very one used in the latest unsolved murder. I'm offering you clean weapons, with twelve bullets in the magazine as well as the one in the chamber, with a decent range and top accuracy. There's no comparison."

"I know. It's the price that's the problem. Can't you go any lower?"

"How much are you willing to pay?"

"No more than six hundred."

I did a quick mental calculation. Perhaps I could get Amaya down to five hundred then sell them to Luis at six-fifty.

"Let me see," I said. "It won't be easy. I'll need an advance."

"No way, Carlos, and for the same reason there's no contract. You bring the rods, and I'll pay in full. But get a move on. If I'm buying from you, it has to be tomorrow."

"I'll get them to you today."

If you feel humiliated and find you want to get heavy with a friend, the best thing to do is to make yourself scarce. Not to mention the fact that the remains of my breakfast were staring up at me from the plate.

Chapter four

At some time between one and one-thirty a.m. on Saturday morning, Jones entered the Malibu Hotel with a blonde-haired, blue-eyed young woman of average height who was wearing trousers and leather boots and jacket. She did not come near the desk but stayed in the shadows. There was nothing unusual about this, as it was common among the type of women who came to this hotel. At three in the morning, the blonde woman came down, but now she had turned into a blond man (apparently it must have been a transvestite). S/he paid for the room and asked for her companion to be wakened at nine.

With regard to the change from woman to man, Juan Avina Recalde, the hotel manager, confirms this was the case and states that he sees them every day, knows their little tricks and is never fooled by them.

At nine that morning Jones's dead body was discovered. He was lying naked on the bed, with a bullet from a .9mm revolver in his head.

The details surrounding the crime lead to the supposition that this came about as the result of an argument between homosexuals.

I slid into the office and took a good look at the woman waiting for me. She was young, fair-haired, shapely and with a look about her that confirmed my theory that the essential thing about a woman is not so much the way she is built but the light shining from her windows. No female is sexy if she goes through life with a face like a funeral.

Estela Lopez de Jones was doing her best to give the appearance of being the grieving wife. She wasn't very good at it. She was too much the TV soap opera heroine about to swoon in despair. I summed her up at once: a cheat. I couldn't see her making that hole in her husband's head, but I could imagine her waiting for the blond criminal stretched out with a glass of whisky and romantic music in the darkness of a plush room, then screwing him till dawn.

I offered her my condolences, asked her to take a seat then searched in my desk drawer for Estela Lopez de Jones's initial statement. It would help me follow the sequence of events and check on any possible discrepancies.

Estela Lopez de Jones was Colombian. Without the make-up, her face looked very different. Her honey-coloured hair was pulled back in a ponytail, her twenty-four years poured into a black tailored suit. She had been living in Los Angeles since the age of nineteen. Before marrying Jones, she had been a checkout girl in a cheap clothes store owned by her father.

I remembered something important. I apologized for keeping her waiting and stepped out of the office.

Laura was on the phone – talking to some boyfriend of hers, to judge by the beatific smile – and wasn't exactly enthusiastic when I asked her to go to the bank for me.

I made out a cheque and left the amount blank. "See how much is in my account and fill it in. Leave five thousand pesos in so they don't close it down. Go on, there's a good girl, Laurita. You can come in an hour later tomorrow. I'll fix it."

Laura is skinny, lazy and spiteful. She can't type a page without making a spelling mistake on every line, and she's always trying to pick up any pair of trousers that passes her desk. With me she's given up. I did her the favour once, but she soon started behaving as though she were my wife, so that was an end to it. She's hated me ever since. Luckily, I'm her superior.

We also have an assistant in the office. What you might call an *office boy*, if that weren't too frivolous and yankee a term for a federal government office in Mexico City. His only talent is never to be around when you need him, and when he is there, to take a whole morning to go to the bank on the corner and back. That's why we call him Silver Bullet; and on rare occasions we succeed in getting him to buy us cigarettes or a sandwich.

Maribel and dona Juana, the lady in charge of cleaning, are also there.

The others are professionals, clerks and cops. And although most of them are hardly even up to running errands, we have to keep up appearances.

I could see the gringo's widow was getting impatient. I excused myself again and began to go through the most important points of her statement with her.

She had been living in the United States for five years and had been married to Jones for eighteen months. Her husband ran a very successful advertising agency. The staff could only feel grateful to him, although in all truth (even though this was hardly relevant) there are always envious and selfish people willing to speak evil of others and to forget the benefits they have received.

"Let's turn to the day of the unfortunate event," I said, to bring her back to business.

"The sixth of January began as a wonderful day," said Estela Lopez de Jones, half-closing her eyes as though evoking a tender memory. "Jones used to spoil me a lot, perhaps to make up for the difference in our ages. And that day he gave me a huge fluffy tortoise as a present. It was so big we joked we could use it as a mattress."

Two images flashed through my mind: Jones making this an erotic Twelfth Night with the gift of a tortoise on which, if he was lucky, he had had his last fuck or, at worst, had imagined doing it; the other, Estela Lopez de Jones naked and in action on the tortoise with the criminal.

"That morning, my husband had work to do," she went on. "We had lunch at a restaurant in the Zona Rosa. In the afternoon he had to see people and more work. He came home at about eight. We had something to eat, then Valadez came. I went to bed at half past ten. I watched TV for a while, then fell asleep. That was the last time I saw my husband alive."

At this point Estela Lopez de Jones appeared to be overcome with emotion and raised her unpainted nails to her blue eyes. Thirty seconds went by, which I used to observe her, light another cigarette and remember that Valadez was someone well worth investigating. He was a Cuban who had left the island when Castro came to power and had lived several years in Miami before settling in Mexico. *He has travelled to the United States ten times in the past three years. He frequents nightclubs and spends a lot of money. He hands out business cards claiming to be a "business and investment adviser" and others where he says he is an "artistic manager". He has been charged five times, twice for fraud and three times for swindling. He has been close to Jones since he arrived in Mexico.* Eventually Estela Lopez de Jones heaved a sigh, said "I'm sorry", reached into her bag for a paper handkerchief to wipe away her tears, then got out a packet of John Players.

"What happened after that?" I asked.

"The next morning I was told he had been found dead in a disreputable hotel."

I looked at the time on my watch, and it was late. A minute afterwards I said goodbye to the widow, warning I would be visiting her again the next day.

*

I bought three dolls and a box of sweets at the Sanborn's opposite the Chapultepec cinema. I

24

could see it already: Gloria would be waiting for me, the most loving and cheerful of women, she would find a moment when the kids weren't around to have a "serious" word and go through the list of all that she needed, combined with an affectionate reproach for spending so much on presents when I could have used the money for repairing the washing machine. I put my foot down on the accelerator. I was in a hurry to be with Gloria and to forget Lourdes.

Chapter five

"Hi there, sir!" Benjamin, Sonia and Berenice greeted me in joyful unison.

They were pleased to see me, though they were pretending the opposite. When they are pleased with me, they call me daddy; when they are upset, they call me sir. I've never had the slightest doubt that it's Gloria who tells them which way to greet me.

After handing over presents and money, after reassuring disbelieving eyes that I would be having dinner there again the next evening, I was daddy once more, I was my love, daddydaddydaddy.

Gloria is a gorgeous woman from Puebla. She is twenty-nine, with fine white skin, auburn hair and huge hazel eyes that are quick to show when she's happy or sad. Her main difference with Lourdes is that sometimes she gives off such a sense of happiness that her face and body positively shine. Lourdes is beautiful too, but she's more edgy and sharp. Her hysterical character is starting to bring wrinkles of disappointment to her face, and she hardly ever laughs spontaneously.

After we had lunch, a chat around the table and then a very satisfactory siesta, at twenty past five in the afternoon I explained to Gloria we had been robbed of a thousand dollars. I led her to the phone and dialled the money exchange number.

"This is Carolina Esparza," she told them, without batting an eyelid. "A cousin of Maria de los Angeles. Is she there?

"I know she doesn't work there any more," she said, all smiles, "but Angeles told me she would be in the office this afternoon sorting out some loose ends. So, well, I don't know . . .

"Yes, I understand," she said, eyes gleaming, squeezing my knee. "Yes, yes . . . No. Don't go to the trouble. I'll get in touch with her myself. Yes, very kind, goodbye."

"They're expecting Rosenthal," she told me. "They said Angeles might possibly be with him."

I called the office. The irony and curtness in Maribel's voice were deliberate. None of the men we can usually call on for a special mission were there. The only males around were Silver Bullet and the Commander. I asked to speak to the boy.

"Listen, but don't speak," I told him. "There's two hundred dollars in it for you. I need you to come with me on an easy job. I'll be waiting for you in twenty minutes on the corner of Reforma and Estocolmo, on the west side. Now get off the phone, but don't hang up. Tell Mirabel I want to speak to the boss. And you, set off to meet me."

"Which is the west side?" asked Silver Bullet.

I explained and repeated how urgent it was. Maribel was playing dumb, giving herself airs and trying to make me feel inferior. I had to be short and sharp to get her to put me through to the Commander.

"For the good of both of us, I hope you're in luck, Officer." The Commander's voice was gloomy and ambiguous, and that "good for both of us" sounded ominous.

*

Silver Bullet dresses as if he were his own father and stuffs his nineteen years into a body typical of someone who gets no exercise and eats nothing but tacos. He has a round face, round eyes and a rat's tail moustache. I could tell he was really excited, because he had his hands out of his pockets.

As he got into my Atlantic, I explained:

"We're going to get some dollars they're trying to steal from the Commander in a money exchange."

"Where are my two hundred?" Silver Bullet demanded.

"We'll also get my commission and your two hundred."

He looked at me doubtfully.

"You're one of us," I said, squeezing his shoulder to make my point. "DO. One hundred per cent Mexican. I specially asked you to come with me because I can recognize a man of action. You can't go on forever spinning cobwebs as a junior."

"As soon as we get out I want my two hundred," insisted Silver Bullet.

Before I left the car in the parking lot I handed

him a Beretta .22 and made it clear it was only to scare people with, not to use. We walked about two hundred feet to the polarized front windows of CAMBIMEX. The door was shut, but I knew there were people working in the offices inside. I rang the bell, and a big guy I had seen there before appeared. Someone they use as a guard when the morning cop goes off duty. I gestured to him in a friendly way through the glass, and he came closer to get a better look. I made more friendly gestures, with the result that he twisted his mouth and used a bunch of keys to turn the lock. He opened the door eight inches, showing he was a novice at this game and was frightened of showing he was worried.

"What is it?" he asked, frowning.

"I've come to see Perez Blanco, the account-ant," I said, still smiling. I always make sure I smile in cases like this. I flashed him my card.

"I'll go and find out if he can see you," the big guy said, trying to shut the door again. He leaned forward and was slightly off balance, giving me the chance to push hard on the door. It flew open and smashed into his face somewhere between mouth and nose. He put his hands up and stumbled back groaning. I pushed him aside and grabbed his revolver from his belt. Silver Bullet showed his ID to a couple and two other men who were passing by the agency. "Police! Move on!" he shouted, then followed me inside.

Two women and four men froze at their desks when we appeared.

In another office I could see Red Rosenthal and another man I took to be Perez Blanco. I walked over to them, checking out an empty cubicle on the way.

"Keep this lot covered!" I shouted to Silver Bullet. "If they cause any trouble, shoot them in the head!"

I don't like being messed about; I get annoyed when I have to go from pillar to post, doing overtime just to get what's mine by right; I hate being made to look a fool. I was furious as I strode into the office. Red got up to come towards me. He was saying something, and waving his arms in the air. I hit him in the face with my gun, and he fell back into his chair. He tried to stand up again, his arm raised in entreaty. I gave him a good kick in the balls, and he fell writhing to the floor squealing like a queer.

The other guy had gone so white he looked pure Aryan. I took a deep breath. I lowered my voice to make it sound even more threatening.

"I want the money! R-i-ght now!"

Paleface, who by now had grasped who I was and who had sent me, tried to calm me down.

"How much do we owe you?"

"A hundred million."

"Ninety million," muttered Red, whose bloody face fitted in even more perfectly with his nickname. "Thirty thousand dollars, which I changed at three thousand, that makes ninety million pesos. I was always going to pay you, but I won't forget this, I can tell you."

Paleface looked at me quizzically.

"It was ninety, but there's another ten in interest because of all the hassle you've put me through to get them," I explained. "You'll make up the difference in a few days. I don't want another word. Either you hand over the money or you're coming with me."

"We'll have to open the safe."

"I'll give you one minute."

While they were getting the money, I took stock of the situation. Beretta in hand, Silver Bullet had the office in his sights. In his other hand he was clutching a bag of crisps. Among the women looking on in terror, I caught sight of Red Rosenthal's secretary-nymphette.

With the money safely in my briefcase, I went over to her. Her pleading eyes showed she had been stripped of all make-up, disdain, all smugness and self-satisfaction. Thanks to the narcotic lucidity of action, I realized that Maria de los Angeles Esparza was no longer the vain little nymph who could look right through me while at the same time inevitably spotting the grease stain on my trousers, but was now a woman who would offer no resistance to whatever I might tell her to do. Hard as a god I came to a halt beside her desk. A brief sob rose in her throat. I tweaked her nipple just once, as hard as I could, and didn't let go until she moaned. I liked seeing tears in her eyes.

We got back into the car without problems. I took seven hundred from a bundle of notes and stuffed them in one of Silver Bullet's pockets.

"There's more than two hundred there," I told him.

"Want some, boss?" Silver Bullet held out the packet of crisps he had found on one of the desks in CAMBIMEX.

*

I felt relaxed and pleased with myself. A job well done, words of praise from a superior and a nice pile of banknotes to keep me warm. All of this contributed to my happy state of mind. I had the Commander eating out of my hand. He passed up on the ten per cent in my favour. So that after paying him his cut and the money I'd given my sidekick, I still made more than four million straight profit.

On my way home I thought I might open a bank account in Lourdes's name. I'd put enough in so she could spend it as she liked, to buy shoes or dresses or perfumes. That would be a nice touch, and a pleasant surprise for her. The truth was I missed her a hell of a lot. I've grown used to her body, her voice, to having her always near.

Seeing what time it was, and considering that nobody seemed to want to pay me overtime, I took some folders with me to look at outside the office. The gringo business was dragging on. I told the boss I'd work on it and he said I needn't bother coming in the next day.

As I was parking outside my home in San Pedro de los Pinos, I could hear the hoarse wail of

Carlos's saxophone. It seems as though at seventeen music is all he wants from life. I gave him a .22 pistol, but he didn't even try it. It's me who has to clean it and oil it every month. I took him to the Plaza Garibaldi to have some fun (despite the fuss Lourdes kicked up!) and to counteract any side-effects of his musical obsession. You don't have to be a reactionary to be worried about the influence all the homosexuals and drug addicts who abound in that profession might have on an adolescent. It was cool. We danced with some of the girls there, and Carlos lightened up enough to say he was completely drunk on three rum and cokes and to tell me I wasn't to worry, he was no queer, but that those mariachis hadn't the faintest idea what proper music was. That's how things stand. I'm just glad he's getting good marks at school. That's hard enough.

I found him wrapped in his sheepskin jacket and with his hair brushed back laboriously with a quiff to make him look like Pajaro Loco. His reply to my greeting was a whirl of the saxophone, so I carried on up to the bedrooms to find Araceli. The apple of my eye was putting on make-up in the bathroom, and she stopped any attempt of mine to get close with a "Hi there, Dad! Don't even think of kissing me!" which pricked my enthusiasm like a balloon and led me to think yet again of that strange universal attitude that women have which means that their attempts to doll themselves up take top priority over everything else, all the problems of the United Nations included.

Araceli is a doll whose beauty makes her father proud. What's worrying is that she's fifteen. I know what men are like, and that's what worries me.

The three of us embarked on a lively discussion as to what nationality restaurant we would choose. We decided we'd stuff ourselves on pasta and stew in a trattoria. The decision put us in a good mood that lasted all night.

I used the meal to set them straight on a few misguided opinions their mother had about me, and my determination to prove her wrong. I encouraged them to be part of my team when they went to see her and to tell her that all the family was anxiously awaiting the return of the queen bee to her hearth and home.

Chapter six

The second beer was cold and delicious. That did not seem so hard to achieve. Not warm or frozen, just cold. It appeared so simple, I was tempted to believe even my own wife could do it.

I checked the guns I had got for Luis: four parabellum Lugers. Beautiful weapons, with well-constructed sights, easy to strip and put together again. Designed to look good in salons and to be used in the muddy fields of Europe. Linked to elegant officers and to the rough hands of German peasants. Antiquities that have elegantly withstood the passage of time, objects a man likes having and using. And compared to all the fancy gadgets on other guns, just right for people who never thought that to hold up a pharmacy you had to be a watchmaker.

I couldn't get anything out of Amaya. The cheapest he was prepared to sell for was 520 dollars each. I told him I'd try to get others at a better price. There's a market for guns, and the good thing is that you don't have to go far to find it. There are so many goods being shifted through the public offices of this country ever day that more than one supermarket chain would be green with envy. From books to drugs, shoes to pornography, everything is bought and sold. Three phone calls, a visit to another office, and I found myself staring at these four beauties, a steal at 450 each, a special price just for me.

"I've got what you ordered," I told him by phone. "Six hundred each, as we agreed."

"I need to see them," Luis cut in.

"I'll be there in half an hour. Have everything ready."

"I'll be expecting you."

I called Estela Lopez de Jones and a voice with a broad Oaxaca accent told me: "Madam is having a bath." I said I would be coming to talk to her in an hour and a half, and the Oaxacan voice replied: "I'll tell the mistress right now, because I'm going out to do the shopping." I imagined a woman of forty-five, weighed down with kids, and innocent enough to give all this information to a stranger. I said that if she was going to tell her straightaway, could she please give me the answer. The answer was "Madam will wait for you at home."

"Forgive me for asking," – sometimes I like to check if my intuition is working properly – "but are you from Oaxaca?"

"Yes."

"Don't be upset, but . . . would you be around forty-five years old?

"I'm eighteen."

"Fine, thanks. Don't forget to remind your mistress I'm on my way."

The business with Luis went as smooth as clockwork. He inspected the wares carefully, then beamed at me. When someone as suspicious as Luis smiles at you, it's because everything is in order, and breakfast is on the house. I guessed he must already have a buyer at a very good price, and that if I had put the pressure on, I could have made more myself.

On my way to Copilco I had an idea. I pulled up alongside the first public callbox. I have a personal test I apply to women who for whatever reason interest me. I call them up, I pant and make obscene noises just like a typical anonymous sexual pervert. In my book, only those women who get angry and insult me are the ones to trust. I've been surprised more than once, which only goes to show how effective the trick is. Every so often I try it on Lourdes and Gloria and am gratified to find myself showered in terrible curses. Lourdes is so vehement, furious and almost delighted as she lays into and humiliates me that I suspect she must know who is making the calls.

Estela Lopez de Jones took the call, so I did my little number, taking care to disguise my voice and its highs and lows because I would be seeing her in a few minutes. She asked twice: "Who's speaking?" and hung up. I called again. Experience has taught me that when a woman receives a porno call the shock and her cultural conditioning always lead her to hang up immediately. If you end the experiment there, all you learn is that they did not think much of it, but you don't get any further than that, nothing you can evaluate or draw conclusions from. She picked the phone up, and I started off with my panting. This time she went on listening. I raised the volume several decibels and began a nose-ear-throat orgasm of Wagnerian proportions. The widow burst out laughing, and I started to cough. "Idiot," she said, still chuckling. I insisted, threatening a second coming. "Idiot," she repeated, in the same amused voice. She laughed some more, said "What an imbecile!" and hung up.

The woman waiting to use the phone looked at me as if I were something dirty squashed on the pavement that might get stuck on her shoe.

That's the risk we run in our profession. I didn't have to reflect too long to decide the result of my test. I think there are six kinds of woman: those who hang up at once; others who listen without saying anything; others who say "idiot-imbecile" but don't seem too upset. Then there are those who get into an exciting conversation that leads nowhere; those who get furious and forget all female decorum; and those who take advantage of any silence to make a date with the anonymous heavy breather. Jones's widow was in the third category: willing to cheat, the repressed orgiastic type, the sort who run rings round their husband.

Pretty much what I had in mind.

*

I stopped at a household goods store and spent twenty minutes choosing an electric oven for Gloria. For some time I'd been thinking of buying one for Lourdes. But all's fair in love and war, and if she was going to walk out on me, there was no way I was going to sing her a love song. When she comes back I'll buy her a microwave. She's going to be sorry for all the evil thoughts she had about Carlos Hernandez.

At the Copilco house I was received by the Oaxacan maid. She had nice teeth and legs, and looked a long way from forty-five, perhaps because all maids are unaware that old age always creeps up on you unseen.

A loose-fitting black sweater and skirt stood guard over Estela Lopez de Jones's consolable body. In the living room three people were engaged in what looked like a conspiratorial meeting. A thirty-year-old couple, so alike they could only be man and wife – grey suit, grey tailored suit; matching tie and dark grey stockings; brown hair and lifeless eyes, both of them formal and polite, complete hypocrites – were presented to me as Jones's accountant and his wife. I knew Valadez from his photo – *Been tried five times. Must have good contacts to still be going around free. The Interior Ministry has its eye on him. One of his known frauds is the habit of pretending to be one of their inspectors in order to extort money from unsuspecting victims.* Having a folder on current cases is useful: that way you know what kind of bastards you are going to run into. The question I wanted to ask Valadez was a simple one: what is the link between a Caribbean fraudster and a rich murdered gringo? Even if I didn't know the Cuban from his photo, I would have recognized him. Impossible not to, with that shiny bald head, the tufts of brilliantined hair above his ears, his scrawny body in a black roll-neck under the grey suit threaded with silver and the wary look he gave me as I walked into the room.

No sooner had we been introduced, than Valadez asked me:

"How is the investigation going, Officer?"

"As you are aware, we are not at liberty to give any details while we are investigating." I was trying to make them understand something people find so hard to grasp: it's the cop who gets to ask the questions.

I spent some time with them, without getting very far. The Cuban said he had been with Jones until eleven o'clock on Friday night. "Listen carefully to what I'm going to say," he told me. "Jones was doing very well in Mexico. He had no enemies. I helped him with contacts and relations. That evening we had a few drinks and talked business. At eleven I left him. That's all there is to it." The accountant and his wife had been to the cinema that night. They saw *Interiors* at the Elektra, and both thought Woody Allen was not what he used to be. According to the accountant, Jones's bank balances were in the black. Satisfactory and growing profits. The Cuban took advantage of this to boast how it was all thanks to his contacts. He managed to get in references to the former Soviet Union and the world situation, and to emphasize that it was thanks to them, the democratic Cubans who had begun the struggle back in 1960, that communism had finally been defeated. "Listen carefully to what I'm going to tell you," he said again. "The bearded one is the toughest nut of all. But one of these days we're going to overthrow him, though as ever it'll be others who take the credit." Estela Lopez de Jones admitted that "very occasionally" her husband "fell back" into the temptation of unimportant adventures, which did not affect the stability of their marriage, since both she and Jones were "modern, broad-minded" people (when she said "broad-minded" I realized that was the expression generally used to sell pornography, and I had a couple of fleeting images of Estela and the tortoise). She considered it impossible for her husband to be mixed up with transvestites. That must be gossip in the scandal sheets.

Convinced I was going to get nowhere if I continued talking to the four of them together, I pretended to write in my notebook, came out with a few routine comments about counting on their collaboration to see justice was done and set up a meeting with Valadez.

Chapter seven

Quasimodo's real name is Jose Miguel Rivas Alcantara, but he's known as Quasimodo because of the enviable gift he has of scaring the pants off everyone. He's a good friend of mine, and, what's more, he owes me a favour. Two years back I testified in his favour in a case of "extortion and abuse of authority", when if someone had believed more in the sanctity of oaths than in those of friendship, things would have gone extremely badly for him.

He greeted me with an enthusiastic display of countless greenish teeth, we clapped each other's hand as though we were beating a drum, then, as we always do when we meet, spent half an hour telling each other news about our colleagues. Quasimodo knew a lot about the rapist cops in Fuentes Brotantes but didn't know a thing about how the wife of one of the big chiefs had been fucking around; he had information about links between commanders and drug runners but none about the row with the President's people. We had a couple of coffees, smoked a few cigarettes, and then I asked him about Valadez. Things only exist if there's a file on them. Quasimodo smiled his Nibelungen smile and went off to find a folder.

*

I called the office from a bar. Maribel's voice sounded warm, but instantly fell the whole length of the thermometer when she heard who was calling.

I asked to speak to Silver Bullet and arranged to meet him at seven at the Insurgentes roundabout.

"I don't know if I can make it . . . I've got a date," Silver Bullet said.

I imagined him on a date with Maribel. I imagined her desperate beside the office boy and enjoyed the thought that the nymphomaniac was going to hate me even more.

"There could be a lot of dough in it," I told him.

"How much?"

"Dunno. That depends on the guy and on us. But it's there for the taking, and if we play our cards right, it could be a lot more than you think."

"The thing is . . . " he stuttered.

"I'll pick you up at seven," I said and hung up. That's what you always have to do in these cases.

Then I called Carlos to find out how he had got on with Lourdes.

"OK," he said, in that flat tone of someone who has no real news.

"What did she say?"

"She said that if you want to talk to her you should have the courage and decency not to send a boy, and that in a few days she's going to take me and Araceli to live with her."

That kid gets to me sometimes.

"Did you tell her I'd paid the school fees, that I did a supermarket shop for six hundred

43

thousand pesos and that our economic situation has improved dramatically?"

"Yes."

"And?"

"She didn't say anything. She just stared at me and said nothing."

"Where's your sister?"

"She went to the cinema with a boyfriend."

"What!"

"Just a joke, boss. She's upstairs, studying. Want me to call her?"

He's got a sense of humour, the criminal. One of these days I'm going to forget he's my son and, instead of laughing, I'll smash his face in.

"No. I'm busy. Tell her I called, and I'll call again. Don't go out, and don't open the door to anybody."

I phoned Gloria and told her I'd be with her around ten.

"Have a cold beer ready for me, and something light to eat. And for dessert, I'll eat you."

"Promises, promises!" she laughed happily. I know that kind of laugh. Like all men, I'm a slave to them.

*

At seven I met up with Silver Bullet. Two days earlier I had asked him as a favour – putting on my best disingenuous face, which brings out the maternal instincts in some women, but apparently doesn't arouse any kind of instinct in office boys – to call by the garage in Buenos Aires street, ask for Kiko and bring me the money he handed over.

"I couldn't go," an imperturbable Silver Bullet forced me to hear.

I decided to be realistic about it.

"Try to go tomorrow. Five per cent for you."

Kiko hands over seven hundred thousand a week (four hundred go straight into the Commander's pocket); in return we turn a blind eye: he has a green light to buy and sell stolen cars and parts – so long as he doesn't get us into any trouble, of course. Kiko hadn't paid for two weeks now, and the Commander was likely to bring it to my attention at any moment. Besides which, all things considered, fourteen days is a long time. If we let three payments slip, he might never pay again. Best to give a bit and avoid all risks.

"How much is in it?" my assistant wanted to know.

"A million four hundred thousand."

"I'll be there tomorrow."

We had a beer in a bar, and I asked him about the date he had postponed.

"Not postponed, lost," Silver Bullet said. "Laura took it really badly. She won't speak to me again."

"Why didn't you stay to see her?" It's always a good thing to test the discipline of your subordinates.

"With Laura I spend money, boss. With you I earn it. And I need lots of money."

"Why do you need lots of money?"

"To take women out."

At half past seven we were in another bar, two hundred yards further on from the first one. At a quarter to eight Valadez arrived, ordered a whisky, and allowed me to pay for it. We smoked a cigarette then I took him out into the street. "I want to show you something I've got in the car," I told him. The Cuban looked nervous. Silver Bullet and I walked along, flanking him on either side, looking serious.

I sat behind the wheel. Silver Bullet sat beside Valadez in the back.

I aimed for dark streets in the Colonia Roma. I wasn't worried about the couples in the shadows: there is no one more concerned with their own business. Twice Valadez asked: "What was it you wanted to show me?" After twice getting silence as the only reply, he didn't open his mouth again.

I parked under a leafy tree and turned round in my seat.

"Look, Valadez . . . " I paused to increase the suspense, and my tone was intended to show him that his situation had got more complicated. It was already a quarter past eight, I had another two appointments, and by ten o'clock I wanted to be with Gloria. I went on: "Let's talk frankly. I've got nothing against you, and I wouldn't want you to come to any harm. I don't know how guilty you are, but you've got mixed up in some dirty business with that friend of yours who pretends to be an Interior Ministry inspector." (When a cop offers the accused the possibility of blaming a third person, he is meant to understand this does not come free of charge.) "You know ministries don't like to be taken for a ride, especially not the people in Interior. We're not accusing you of anything yet, and I'd be very pleased to hear you demonstrate your innocence. Off you go."

Valadez cleared his throat nervously, trying to give the impression he was laughing with relief, friendship and self-confidence.

"Oh, so that's what's worrying you! Listen carefully to what I'm going to say!" He was recovering his composure as he went along, while I was deciding that the next time he told me to "listen carefully" I'd give him a good punch in the stomach. "Look, it was all a joke. Someone I know made up the whole thing so he could collect a bad debt. All I did was go with him. My friend introduced me as an agent from Interior, and the other guy paid up. I never even said I was one. That's all there was to it. Just a joke."

"I don't have a copy of the penal code on me," I replied, "but I'll send you one in jail. Read it carefully, and you'll see how many years you could get for abuse of position and authority, for intimidation and fraud, extortion and a few other offences that your 'joke' might involve. That's the problem with our lawmakers: they don't have much sense of humour. Who's your accomplice?"

"Gentlemen! . . . You're putting me in an awkward position here! He's a good person, and I wouldn't want him to think I'm getting him in trouble. And he's not my accomplice, because we

47

haven't done anything wrong. Although perhaps my associate did take things a little too far. Perhaps he did get a little out of control when I wasn't around to keep an eye on him."

I sat looking at him.

"His name is Osvaldo Cruz." The voice is the mirror of the soul as well, and the Cuban's sounded weak. "Ever since I came to Mexico, I've cooperated with the authorities. I have good friends in government."

"Where does he live?"

"Apartment 2, 20 Cinco de Febrero Street, in Colonia Portales. I wouldn't like this to get out. We're all here to add our grain of sand, to help justice and democracy."

"You're done for, asshole!" Silver Bullet was quaking with indignation: there's an actor hidden in every cop. "We're going to take you in for interrogation, and you're going to tell us everything, including how many hairs there are in Fidel Castro's beard! You'll rot in solitary while we haul in that damned accomplice of yours!"

"You can't do that to me, Officer! I'm on your side! At the very least I have the right to a lawyer!"

As was only proper, this plea was aimed at me.

"We'll do what the Commander here decides is right," I explained, nodding at Silver Bullet.

"By the time we've finished with you, there won't be much left to drag to a lawyer." Silver Bullet was tougher than Bogart and Dirty Harry put together. "You've been stealing and dragging the name of a government department through the mud! I bet you don't even pay your taxes! In case you didn't know it, asshole, in this country you have to pay taxes whenever you do business!"

You could say a lot of things about the Cuban. But no one could ever accuse him of being slow on the uptake.

"Perhaps there's some way of coming to a reasonable arrangement?" he said wearily.

The stage was set. I spoke the prologue.

"I've got a murder case to solve," I said. "I've got more things to attend to, and my family is waiting for me for dinner. I'll walk to the corner, and when I get back we'll go wherever the Commander has decided."

I lit a cigarette and stretched my legs. I would willingly have changed places for half an hour with one of those guys I saw being made love to without embarrassment but with intense pleasure. As though they deserved it, the bastards!

When I got back to the car I switched on the engine. The faces reflected in the rear-view mirror told me everything was fine.

"We're going to Colonia Cuauhtemoc," Silver Bullet said. "It's near where you're going, Officer. Go down Florencia, cross Reforma and take the first street parallel on the left."

Five minutes later and I left them outside Valadez's apartment. I don't like leaving Silver Bullet to work on his own for the same reason I don't like my daughter going out with boyfriends. Both of them are growing up, I know, and have to face the realities of life, but whenever I see them struggling with temptation I get the gut feeling that at any moment there could be a catastrophe. Of course, if Araceli succumbed, it would be far worse. With Silver Bullet there's always the option of crushing his balls and sending him to hospital for the rest of his life. It's a possibility he understands, because I've warned him of it several times. But what can you do with a lost childhood? What can you do with that first time, when you know it's bound to be followed by a second time, and after that by all the numbers in the world? It's hard. I'm not ready yet to become the father of a woman.

As far as the Cuban was concerned, I had no option. If I got directly involved in this "Let's Share the Loot" operation, I would lose my moral authority for the murder investigation. Experience has taught me not to mix work and business. Even in the case of someone who has been so underhand, who you're doing a favour by not throwing them in the slammer.

*

I headed for the Zona Rosa to see the Three Marias. Who was it who named them after a constellation? ... I've no idea. Perhaps they themselves did, with that passion all whores have for artistic names. Perhaps they saw themselves as stars coming down to the city to bring a light to the heart of the sad and lonely; or maybe it was a client of theirs, some "mister" with a superficial knowledge of Mexican folklore. Or it might even have been me, as I was linked more closely than anyone to the three sisters' talents.

Three years earlier, when Rosario started working at home in San Pedro de los Pinos, she never said a word. Three months had gone by before I even became aware of her existence. Then one day I started looking at her and discovered a pleasant face and well-built body. I'm not one of those slimeballs who think that by paying a minimum wage they not only get a shiny clean house but have found themselves a free sex slave into the bargain. All I did was look at her from time to time. It all started when Lourdes went to visit a relative in Morelia for a week. Carlos and Araceli left for school, and Rosario was on her own in the house for several hours. During the first few days there was her body and there was my temptation. (Something similar happened to Saint Anthony.) But nothing would have happened if I hadn't got drunk and lost control. I don't usually drink too much, although like every son of Darwin I like to get a skinful now and again. I hardly ever do so during the day, and whenever I have, it's brought trouble. The fact was I arrived home pretty drunk only to find Rosario in a blouse that left her shoulders bare and revealed the top of her juicy little apples. What follows is a jumbled picture: talking to her, making her laugh, playing with her, chasing her, cornering her in the bedroom, tearing off her clothes. I was too excited, and came before I could even get inside her. Then there's a depressing scene: the girl cries and you feel ashamed for behaving like an animal and still more ashamed you couldn't do it. I ended up giving her a load of money and succeeding in calming her down. The next day I came back stone sober and gave it to her properly. Realizing she wasn't a virgin reassured me a lot.

When Lourdes got back, not only was Rosario saying nothing, but I was silent too. And since in certain matters my wife is a better bloodhound than the entire Mexican police force, she said nothing either but within three days had kicked the maid out. I felt sorry for her, and a bit guilty too. I found her three or four jobs, but they didn't work out. I lost sight of her for a month. By the time I met her again she was on the streets and having trouble with a pimp who beat her. I had to break his leg to get him to leave her in peace. I put Rosario in touch with some girls who worked for themselves. As time went by, her work inevitably led to other problems: permits, health checks and other hassles. I got into the habit of helping her. Rosario ended up bringing her sisters to the city and passing me my cut every month out of sheer gratitude.

I would never have taken it, but I realized this helped her feel more protected and less in my debt. And I've never accepted her offers of payment in kind. I've only very occasionally tried something from her delicatessen counter that I couldn't get from Lourdes or Gloria, given their tendency to prefer routine and a classical approach. What I could not avoid was the

Commander muscling in. He's the one in charge, so he gets to hear these things. And he likes to employ one of the basic principles of public service: the one which states that any business or money a public servant manages to get his hands on beyond his salary has to be shared with his boss. I don't like the idea, just as I don't like pollution or water shortages. The Commander is over sixty; he's a grandfather and doesn't have much luck with the ladies, so perhaps that's why he is so interested in payment in kind. Once a month I have to organize him a session with the Three Marias. Then, of course, along with a guest he brings with him, I find myself forced to take part in order to prevent the Commander getting ideas above his station or deciding to take on the protection himself.

The three girls work from the Oasis Bar in the Calle Hamburgo, the Boboli Bar in the Plaza Florencia Hotel and other dark corners in the neighbourhood.

At the entrance to the Oasis I found two drug dealers I know tossing coins under the bar's red neon light. I asked after the Three Marias, and they sent me to the Boboli.

The Plaza Florencia is a typical Zona Rosa hotel specializing in tourists who pay dollars. The Boboli is a cellar that operates as the hotel's function room. That's where breakfasts and dinner dances are organized for foreign families to enjoy the exotic side of local life at a favourable exchange rate. Some nights too it's where groups of single men come to partake of special services. That's where the Three Marias and other nocturnal butterflies come in.

I asked the receptionist if I could talk to Rosario. She disappeared inside and reappeared a minute later with a shimmering panther with shiny black curls, a model's make-up and four-inch high heels, all the vitality and sexuality that can be poured into 123 pounds, which, as I looked more closely, I identified: it was Rosario.

"What's up, big man?" she said, giving me an affectionate peck on the cheek.

Conclusion: anybody likes a neat piece of ass, and a full set of mammaries is a joy to behold, but what a man really wants is a woman who smiles at him, kisses him on the cheek and gently tells him a white lie by calling him big man.

"Just come to see you, so you won't forget me," I told her.

"I haven't got anything at the moment, but there's lots around," Rosario said, a dialectic look on her face. "All I earned last week has gone, but there'll be plenty for both of us. Right now I'm with the stupidest gringo I've ever met. And let me tell you: one, I've met a lot of gringos, and two, gringos in general are the stupidest people of all."

I study law; I'm going to be a judge one day; I have almost two thousand books in my library. I stared at Rosario and resolved not to try to explain to her that being smart is for gypsies, it's all that's left to those of us who are really in the shit, whereas a chubby freckled little gringo who's been brought up on a diet of proteins and computers doesn't need to be smart at all. He's the one who'll always be the manager and owner of the factory, the one who employs whole teams of smart people like us to work for him.

"What time tomorrow can I see you?" I sighed.

"I don't know if I'll be here," she said, flashing her teeth. "The gringo wants to take me to Taxco and Valle de Bravo."

Not being a gringo, I frowned.

"As soon as you get back, come and find me," I said, pointing at her. "I want to hear from you within two days."

Rosario clung onto my arm, rubbed herself against me, purred:

"Don't be angry, big guy. Everything will work out fine."

How do they manage to change like that in just three years? I'll never know.

I called home to make sure everything was all right. My kids were fighting over the next TV programme: they said they had eaten well, and I didn't doubt it. Next I phoned Gloria to tell her I'd be with her in an hour.

"What's for dinner?"

"Steak, guacamole and salad."

"And beer?"

"A six-pack."

Even though I hadn't said a word, sleeping with her two nights running was a clear sign. Gloria was going to try all her tricks to soften me up. I couldn't avoid it and didn't want to even if I had been able to.

I had one more thing to do before my day was done.

Chapter eight

Cruz turned out to be a hard nut: tough and booze-sodden, one of those who refuse to cooperate. He opened the door four inches, enough for me to make out his furtive animal face and the mop of hair sprouting in thick swirls from just above his eyebrows.

Realizing there was a cop outside and trying to slam the door in my face combined in a single thought and action. I stuck my foot in the crack to stop him, and although my foot came out of it badly, I was stronger than he was, and managed to push my way in.

I showed him my badge with my left hand, keeping my other hand on the butt of my regulation pistol. Cruz collapsed into a chair and did nothing but grunt unintelligibly for a couple of minutes.

The place displayed all the charm of a typical bachelor's apartment: bottles, clothes and newspapers strewn all over the floor; an inch of dust on any object an unwary visitor might touch; the stale smell of dirt, urine, alcohol, tobacco, marijuana and fetid underwear. All of this protected from environmental pollution by firmly shut windows.

I didn't think there was much possibility of getting anything out of this ape. If he hadn't got such valuable information, I would have made do with giving him a good kick in the balls for his bad manners, and gone off to sleep with Gloria.

Instead, I took out Jones's photo and said:

"You threatened this man and pretended to be an Interior Ministry agent in order to blackmail him."

Cruz spat between my shoes and replied:

"Fucking gringo faggots! They think they're God's gift, but all they do is come down here to Mexico and steal our fucking dough!"

"Hmm. So you decided to give him a fright because he was mixed up in shady business."

"Why don't they all just go back to their own fucking country!"

"And make a bit of dough while you were at it."

"No, whaddya . . . "

Cruz was not someone it was easy or interesting to talk to. Unlike his associate, who was quick to seize what was going on, he behaved like a chimpanzee on the defensive. His replies consisted of a mixture of vague generalizations; empty phrases passed off as answers to specific questions; insults intended to demonstrate rejection, denial or disagreement; and monosyllables in a kind of primitive tribal language aimed at protecting the speaker and confusing the questioner.

I considered hauling him in and softening him up in solitary for the night, but it was already well past ten (I'd like to know who else works all day and is still working at ten at night . . . just so that the citizens of this fine country can hold the opinion that the police do not deserve the meagre wages we're paid) and I was desperate to get back, eat, drink a couple of beers and go to bed. So I came straight to the point:

"Listen, asshole. You're breaking the law, and that's very bad. I've no intention of wasting the night on you. So either you tell me right now what you were up to and make me an offer, or I can throw you in the slammer and you can think it over as long as you like. We've got special holes for people like you. By the time you get out you'll be so old you won't even remember your name."

It sounded good, but it didn't work.

"You're fucked, you son of a bitch!" the ape replied, even angrier than I had been. "I'm the brother-in-law of a four-star general, and the Under-secretary of the Interior Ministry is my godfather! Try anything with me, and you're a dead man! It's up to you . . . "

Cruz was raising the stakes, and he knew it. I had no way of guessing whether this creep was simply friends with a patrolman, or if he dined every Friday in the Presidential Palace at Los Pinos. It's a classic criminal ploy: if the shadow of a doubt arises, go for it. And if you do, the one who's the toughest, the one with the most skill and powers of persuasion is likely to win out. Then again, however much you'd like to be somewhere else, staring at some other ugly mug, doing something else altogether, you're in the game now, and there's no quitting.

"Get dressed and bring your ID," I said, seeing Cruz was wearing pyjama trousers and a filthy T-shirt. "You're coming with me. Once you're safely inside we'll give your brother-in-law and your godfather a call."

Cruz grunted and stared at me, itching for a fight. I moved my hand to my waist and lifted my gun an inch out of its holster. He stood up. I wanted to do the same, but I would have lost authority if I didn't go on being calm. From the red mist in my host's eyes and the way he bared his teeth at me, I could tell he might attack at any moment. I stayed put, because that's the next move in the game.

"You'll regret this for the rest of your life, you fucking clown!" Cruz threatened me.

"I'll give you five seconds, then I'm going to get angry."

Cro-Magnon man made for a chest of drawers. As he turned away from me, I quickly pulled out my gun and aimed at the middle of his back. He opened the top drawer, took out a crumpled shirt and laid it on top of the chest. He felt inside the drawer again, and a second later a hail of bullets flew over my head and crashed into the wall and furniture behind me. I put four shots into his chest and one in his forehead. I didn't stop firing until he dropped his weapon.

Conclusion: apart from the penal code, self-defence and other legal justification, the truth is that nailing someone who is trying to kill you is very satisfying. I'm no sadist, and it's not just me. I've asked several colleagues, and they all say the same. It's a question of biology, some sort of memory from our jungle past: we've been challenged and we have come out on top; they tried to defeat us, but we defeated them. There's also a psychological element to it: we have affirmed our personality, we're not as useless as others would have us believe, or even as we ourselves think – that is, in those brief moments when we don't consider ourselves sheer geniuses.

You feel alive, and that doesn't happen every day. I feel it when a dame starts to groan with passion, or when I solve a case neatly, when I'm on holiday or, like now, when I send a son of a bitch who thought he could pull one over on me to the cemetery.

I was on the ground floor of a four-storey block. I could hear sounds and voices, see lights being switched on and off. Clear signs that the whole building was aware that something had happened in Osvaldo Cruz's apartment.

There was nothing else for it, so I called the police. But before that I switched all the lights on and carried out a rapid search. I found a stash of money and a handful of jewels hidden at the bottom of a drawer. I chose a necklace for Lourdes and a pair of earrings for Gloria no one would notice. The main thing always is not to take anything that might affect the investigation. I stared at the rest of the jewels for a good while then picked out a bracelet about half an inch thick that looked as if it was made of gold. I put it in my pocket.

When the detectives arrived, I briefly explained what had happened. The 'tecs stared at the stash of jewels, stared at me as if they wanted to search me, then let me go after I swore I would give them a proper statement the next day.

Some days and nights never seem to end. I set off through Tlalpan, heading for the viaduct, but before I had gone two hundred yards I knew it was too late to go to Mixcoac. I stopped at an open store and bought a few tins of seafood, ham, cheese, sausages, bread, cigarettes and a bottle of "traditional Bacardi" rum. I decided I'd eat with my friend Rivas Alcantara, who lives in Colonia Viaducto Piedad. He's someone everyone is scared of for the same reason they're scared of spiders. He owes me a favour, and he's in charge of an amazing archive, where there's more information than a man can absorb without gossiping about it from time to time with a friend he can trust.

I cruised around the neighbourhood until I found his address. I saw several cops on the lookout in their cars with the lights out; and plenty of people who would look a lot better behind bars. When it comes to physiognomy, I'm with Lombrosio. Forgetting Quasimodo, who's a friend of mine, in this city some of the drunken bums you see roaming around have mugs which immediately tell you that if they haven't just killed a man or raped a woman or robbed a store, they'll be doing so in the next quarter of an hour or so. That's what happened with Cruz. My expert eye was not mistaken, and if I hadn't been forewarned and had my gun trained on his midriff, I'd be the one dead right now, and the 'tecs would have shared out my watch and the few banknotes I had on me. I saw quite a few delinquents of around the same age as Carlos behaving stupidly and noisily under the yellow lights on street corners; and I saw young girls like Araceli who ought to have been at home rather than rubbing themselves up against some guy or other in dark doorways. I found a public phonebox and called San Pedro de Los Pinos. It was engaged, so I knew at least one of my kids was where they should be. Fifty per cent of my worries were over. I called Quasimodo's apartment, and no one answered. I felt frustrated at seeing the place in darkness and my friend obviously not there. I called the Archive, and Quasimodo answered. That man works as if he were well paid, or didn't want to go home. I told him I'd call in on him, and drove off again as if I too were paid to do so.

*

"This is interesting, Carlitos!" We were finishing our meal; I had managed to get through to my kids and tell Gloria that something unexpected had come up. A few men and women were walking along the aisles of the Archive, adding to the feeling of museum and eternity that is typical of temples to memory. "So the Jones case led you to Cruz . . . Let me tell you: we're surrounded by useless cretins who don't know their arse from their elbow."

"What are you talking about?"

"I don't mean you." Quasimodo waved his arm in the air, as if to fend off any protest on my part. "Do you want to know the secrets behind a proper investigation?"

I bit my tongue. At eleven-fifty at night, after a day working like a galley-slave, instead of being flat out on my bed with a glass of rum and a cigarette, reading a novel or watching a film on TV, here I was wasting my time on a guy with a face like a cockroach who was insisting on showing off. Quasimodo had carried on chewing the whole time as he listened to what had happened at the Portales building and now was using his home advantage to teach me lessons about police procedure.

"If you would be so kind as to explain . . . "

"This is the first," my friend said, patting the folders he had shoved to the side of his desk to make room for the ham, sausages and so on. "A good archive: proper files with reliable information. Get everything down on paper, because you never know what might come up. The second is knowing about the butterfly effect, and the concatenation of contradictions."

"Meaning . . . ?"

"Meaning that everything is related to everything else."

The Quasimodo show. And Hernandez the patient spectator. What else could I do . . . ?

"So what?"

"So, Jones is in another file, related to another unsolved death."

That was different. I almost forgot about being annoyed.

"Why didn't you say so?"

"Because I don't work as a fortune-teller any more. You only asked about Valadez."

He was right.

"Tell me."

My friend served two large glasses of rum, stood up and said: "I'll go and fetch some ice." He stopped off on the way to talk to a well-endowed black-haired woman. I passed the time contemplating a stack of archives that reached the ceiling and turned at a right angle out of his office, continued as far as the eye could see on through other offices, and possibly even reached out into the street or into a tunnel, perhaps even as far as the Interior Ministry or the Presidential Palace itself. When he came back with lots of ice and a black folder under his arm Quasimodo gave me a brief summary of the notes in the Jones file. It was a delicate matter, and the high-ups were keeping tabs on it, apparently at his embassy's request.

I listened; filled the glasses; smoked my cigarette.

"What exactly your man has been up to isn't clear," Quasimodo concluded. "But it stinks to high heaven, I can tell you. Officially, his job is filming ruins and pre-Hispanic sites, but he spends his whole time looking for whores in all the agencies."

Heavy stuff. I tried to bring it back to my own area.

"What have Cruz and Valadez got to do with it?"

"Valadez worked with him, he was supposed to be his representative for some deals. Cruz is from a very different world. It's impossible to imagine him with Jones. However . . . "

He pored over the black folder.

"Yes . . . ?"

"A little over a month ago they were together in the Royal Hotel. They had a meal and were arguing. They both got very heated."

"Who supplied the information?"

"Someone."

"Was Jones being watched?"

"What do you think?"

"Do you know anything about that blond transvestite who was with Jones the night he was killed?"

Quasimodo subjected me to another display of his ravaged smile.

"That's your case, Carlitos. What I've said has to do with this one," he said, tapping his file marked "Victoria Ledesma" with a coffee-coloured finger. "It's all top secret. I can't make any photocopies or give you information from it, or even let you take a peek at it. But now I'm off to get the ice cubes for my last drink. I'll be back in exactly fifteen minutes."

We synchronized our watches. Quasimodo left the file on the desk and walked out holding the Tupperware still full of ice.

Jose Miguel Rivas Alcantara may not be Kevin Costner, and now I come to think of it, I've no idea how he ever attracts any women, but he's a good and grateful friend.

*

As I had thought, it was too late to visit Gloria. Despite feeling half dead, to have felt alive once that day was quite enough for me. So I arrived back at San Pedro de los Pinos after half past one, and found Carlos and Araceli stretched out on my bed, guzzling the mysterious contents of various bags of snacks while they watched a rock programme on TV. I reminded them that they would be spending the next day with their mother, that the next day had already begun and chased them out of my room.

I fell asleep covered in crumbs, content for one night at least not to be covered in kisses.

Chapter nine

I got up early to write some letters: I wrote five different ones to Lourdes. At around nine I had a look at the paper. I finished my beer and the can of snails in chilli sauce I hadn't been able to resist buying in the supermarket. I'd never tasted snails, and when I saw the can within my reach I thought that, given their gastronomic prestige, the least I could do was to try some. Now I've done it: they're nauseating. I ate all of them just to be sure I could say I had eaten snails.

I put the necklace in an envelope and handed it to Araceli.

"This is for your mother," I said. "Give her this as a present."

"Nothing else?" Araceli had seen me struggling with pen and paper and doubtless was expecting a sentimental missive from Papa to Mama.

"Give her a kiss from me," I replied, convinced there are silences that triumph where words fail.

As my children were leaving, I picked up the phone. Maribel's mocking voice again reminded me that she was really getting on my nerves. The boss wanted to talk to me.

"You've been on holiday for a week investigating that gringo's death, and your reports are a load of bullshit," the Commander barked. "Are you going soft in the head, or do you think I'm stupid?"

"No, boss, how can you think that? Give me a few more days – I'm on the right track. Oh, and I've got something for you," I added, waving goodbye to the bracelet that looked as if it was made of gold.

"You've got till Friday. Not a day longer. And come and see me at the office today."

"Yes, boss."

It was half past nine. I called Jones's accountant and made an appointment with him for eleven. Another beer gave me the strength to go and make my statement about Cruz's death. Luckily, I had enough petrol, and it only took me the usual length of time to get across a city choked by demented traffic. There are a lot of hysterical drivers in the Mexican capital. And even though I have certain advantages, because if any asshole gets in my way I point my gun at his head and convince him to let me through, it's always hard to get anywhere on time.

The detectives were cool. No one mentioned the stash of jewels. Some magician had made it disappear from the investigation. I mentioned the case of the gringo and said it was out of my hands. They got me to sign a few bits of paper and let me go, with the usual warnings about the course of the investigation and making sure I was available if called upon.

*

The Commander was having a political brunch at the Diplomatico.

Maribel and Laura stared at me, whispered to each other and giggled like idiots.

The accountant was sitting there, as depressed as any innocent person would be at having to spend the morning in a police station waiting room.

"Just a moment. I'll be right with you," I told him, sweeping past. I went to see the three lads in maintenance.

"I've got a number three," I explained. "We've got to play the 'Tell Me What You're Keeping Hidden' game."

"Is he guilty?"

"No, but we need to find out what he knows."

"How much?"

"Forty each."

"Eighty."

"Sixty."

"You're on."

I gave them instructions while they took off their overalls and put on uniforms that were too big for them. In the maintenance room they keep cast-off clothes and unusual sizes. I left them tidying away their gadgets and setting the scene: bare cables, iron gloves, sharp instruments. The maintenance boys never hurt a fly, but they're great for scaring witnesses who need a bit of encouragement to cooperate.

As I was taking him into the interrogation room, the accountant was desperately trying to get me to speak. He wanted to know why I had called him in, what it was all about and so on. As though I were working for him. I said nothing and allowed him to get even more scared, if possible.

I sat him down opposite the man at the typewriter and called the other one aside to give him details about Mr Accountant's state of mind.

"I'll come and get him in half an hour," I said.

"By then he'll be ripe for you."

I went back to the office, where I had a job to do.

Maribel was still looking at me as if she were Lucretia Borgia and I was the monk responsible for cleaning the Vatican toilets.

"I need to get some papers from the boss's office," I told her, smiling my best seductive smile.

"No chance. The boss is out," she replied, dry as a prune.

"I know he's out. That's why I'm asking you to open it for me. I've already spoken to him," I insisted.

The girl from Veracruz looked up at me suspiciously, but picked up the bunch of keys.

Inside the office, I blocked the door.

"I've got half an hour," I told her. "Should we go to a hotel, or do you prefer here?"

She glanced down at her watch. I pushed her onto the couch. By the time I emerged twenty minutes later, I had one less problem. I could not work out why the Commander's secretary was still eyeing me with an air of triumph.

I didn't deign to pay attention to anyone in the

office. That was for Maribel to see to: she was the one who had been stuffed. I went to find the accountant.

He was a sorry sight. Fortunately for him, I arrived just in time to rescue him. I got angry with the lads: "Can't you idiots tell the difference between a criminal and an honest man!" But I kept them close by so that our witness would not be tempted to go back on what he had already given away. Ten minutes' chat, with a cup of coffee and cigarettes, was enough to supply me with very valuable information.

Chapter ten

The gold bracelet – real or not? (I never got to find out) – passed from my hand to the desktop and, from the top, passed into a drawer that was immediately locked. Through a flap in the purple-green folds of his face, the Commander was scrutinizing me.

I was thinking that if anyone stuck a fork in his pupils, all that would come out would be pure alcohol, a geyser of black-label whisky, pools of seven-year-old rum, gushing falls of aged tequila, a river of Rhine wine, a sea of burgundy. For their benefit I drew a picture of the situation, emphasizing my belief that Jones's real business had to do with hetero- and homosexual sadistic pornography. The gringo had set himself up in Mexico because here all that filth was a novelty. And because no one knew of its existence, no one bothered him. Here in Mexico we're still at the innocent stage of sucking tits and anal sex. In the United States, on the other hand, they're used to sadism, pornography with animals and children, films of real deaths. Two whores, Alejandra Aguado and Berta Sanchez by name, had filed a complaint that Jones had them brutally whipped while they were being filmed and had drugged them and forced them to take part in orgies with more than ten men. The women had not followed this up, and nobody knew where they were now. Six months earlier, Jones had contracted Victoria Ledesma, a nineteen-year-old prostitute from Sinaloa, as a model for a shoot in Teotihuacan. The film was made. Twelve minutes of panoramic views, aerial shots and close-ups with the girl in various parts of the ruins, with clay flute music and a supposedly poetic commentary. Two months later the body of Victoria Ledesma was dug out of a rubbish dump by a dog. Her breasts had been hacked off, there were stab wounds all over her body, and several specimens of semen in each of her orifices. Nothing could be proved, but the investigation led the police to suspect Jones's involvement. But he had good contacts in his embassy, and the quality of the evidence against him was such that it was not thought worthwhile to arrest him. The case was still open, and now Jones's death suggested a fresh line of approach. I told the Commander about Valadez and his dealings with Cruz. And about Cruz's links to Jones, which only made sense if we assumed the Cuban had told Cruz about Jones's shady business, and Cruz was the one doing the blackmailing.

"Where did you get the information about Jones?" The Commander put on his best public prosecutor scowl to cross-examine me.

I did not want to get Quasimodo mixed up in this, so I made up some comments made by the detectives when they questioned me over Cruz's death, suggestions from Estela Lopez de Jones and Valadez and, above all, what the deceased Cruz had told me: all of which, thanks to my brilliance as an investigator, had led me to build up a picture which until now only I had been able to see, but which I was happy to put at his – ruthless pursuer of justice and truth – disposition.

The Commander chopped the air with a "cut the crap" gesture and said:

"Tell me about the man or woman who was with Jones in the hotel on the night of the crime."

I admitted I hadn't made much progress on that front. I did not admit I had not even visited the hotel. The fact was I hadn't had the time. But who can tell their boss that?

"You investigate everything, except for what's most important," the Commander snorted. Like all bureaucrats who spend their lives with their arses stuck to a seat, he thinks he's an expert and has the right to demand everything. "If Jones was filming pornography, and let me tell you that a bit of a thrashing on a backside and a few groans may be exciting, but the idea of filming someone's death sounds like a drunk's delirium to me ... who would buy that kind of thing, eh? Tell me, who would run the risk of spending a lifetime in jail for something that can't be that profitable anyway? ... They'd have to be not only the most heartless criminal in the world, but the stupidest into the bargain." He pointed his boss's finger at me, the finger of a schoolmaster pointing at a backward pupil, of a cop accusing his good-for-nothing subordinate, and went on: "As I was saying, if that guy was filming pornography, he must have worked with other people. Actors, a lighting crew, and so on. Why don't you try to find them, Officer, or do I have to tell you how to do your job?"

He's like a father to me, that's why I hate him so much.

"I already have, of course, boss." I improvised a little, using some of the information the accountant had given me. Jones's accounts were all in order. The filmings were carried out in accordance with all the legal and union requisites. He took on professional people and did it all the Mexican way. That was his cover.

"If you're talking about cover, first you have to show the pornography exists."

"I can show lots of suspicious facts: the complaint of sadistic treatment by two women; the link to a prostitute whose mutilated dead body has been found; and underworld rumours about the true nature of Jones's business." (I was spinning a yarn: nobody was going to say some of it wasn't true.) "We've established that Jones did not need a crew to film with, he did his own lighting and camerawork. He has a processing lab in his home. I haven't seen it yet, but I will do later today. Sometimes the gringo employed would-be actors nobody ever saw. They came from Tijuana and San Diego."

"What else . . . ?"

"Nothing. I'm working on my own and making

more progress than if I was part of a team. The gringo was killed, and I'll bet it wasn't because the murderer – man or woman – didn't appreciate the quality of his films."

There was something the boss didn't like. I could tell because the mottled flaps closed still further.

"Tell me about Cruz. He was a good witness. Why did you have to kill him?"

As I said, he's like a father to me.

"Because if I hadn't, he would have killed me."

"Fine. Don't worry. I'll make sure you don't have any problems. It's a clear case of self-defence. We won't allow anyone to suggest other-wise." The Commander was starting to defend me – implicitly, that meant I was guilty. I suddenly realized we were both behaving like cats on the prowl. "What we've got to worry about are the complications in the Jones case. He had friends in his embassy, and they are pressing for the case to be closed. Whether it's cleared up or not, they want it closed. There are questions of reputation and cross-border relations involved. We're the DO here, not illiterate patrolmen. That means we're supposed to use our heads. Justice has never been an exact science, Officer. It's all about relations between people and between countries, and higher interests that have to be treated with caution. Don't forget NAFTA and the foreign debt."

We carried on like this for a few more minutes, playing verbal ping-pong, swapping promises and threats of blackmail until the Commander gave me three days to wrap the case up, told me to give him a daily report and asked if I needed anything.

"Yes, I do," I said. "I want Estela Lopez de Jones's phone tapped, I want a twenty-four-hour watch on her house, and four men in two cars to tail people."

The boss returned to his speciality: adopting a funereal look and saying "no". He blathered on about austerity, budgets and multitasking and ended by saying I knew what to do about the phone tapping, and "talk to someone in the office about the tailing".

Frankly, the Mexican police is run by fools. How can anyone work in conditions like that?

Chapter eleven

Bucareli is a tough, ugly, dirty, polluted, noisy neighbourhood. The day cholera breaks out in Mexico City, it will start in Bucareli, among all the bums and stray dogs, the hordes of rats and mountains of waste paper. But with Bucareli, what you see is what you get. In spite of all the preserved colonial lanes of Coyoacan, all the shopping malls being built in the four corners of the capital, all the fake European nooks and crannies invented for the tourists, Mexico City is a rough place. There's little room in Bucareli for daydreamers, and a cop is unlikely to forget what he's there for.

By my second tequila I had the case solved. The key was a blonde woman who could switch easily to being a blond man. Everyone knows the best place to hide a tree is in a forest. And hadn't we had a blonde woman in front of our faces the whole time? And didn't that woman have a difficult relationship with Jones? Hadn't I seen with my own eyes – with these eyes that devour women – how she could put up her hair in a bun? She could do exactly the same wearing the collar of a leather jacket turned up . . . the man at the hotel said he had seen a transvestite. But, apart from the amazing facility witnesses have to transform mulattoes into Negroes, Peruvians into Japanese, a transvestite is simply a man imitating a woman – and isn't it easy to confuse a man who imitates a woman and a woman imitating a man? Estela Lopez de Jones had been clever. She had done her number in a cheap hotel, and counted on people following their normal line of thinking and being unable to link a decent woman with a hotel used by prostitutes, allowing her to create the illusion that there was someone else involved. Then she transformed this other woman into a man, leaving the narrow logic of any observer in a spin. Her motives were hatred and greed. Hatred, because of what the accountant told me, but I didn't pass on to the Commander; greed because if that son of a bitch gringo was going around snuffing people and filming it, the only possible explanation was that someone was paying at the very least a million greenbacks for each of those "emotional hits". Somewhere, perhaps in a Swiss bank, there must be a deposit in Jones's name that would allow anyone not to have to worry about working ever again.

Not bad going for a shop assistant in a cheap store. My job was to catch her.

I called in at several bars before I found him. Sitting with a plateful of pork tacos and a mamey juice, Silver Bullet looked pleased with himself. When he saw me, he ordered a beer from the waiter. This pleased me, because it's always nice to see one's disciples are learning and discover they know it's important to keep their superiors happy.

I had to give him instructions about the way to deal with the Cuban, so I sat on a stool next to him. I began by downplaying what he had achieved so far, to keep him in his place. Nothing is easier for people than to give themselves airs. Everybody seems to need to feel they are in charge of something, to boast "It was me who did it", "I'm the number one." So I confirmed he would get his share of twenty per cent, and not the thirty per cent he was asking for, and informed him that yours truly had been busy adding noughts to the right-hand side of that twenty. I told him about Cruz and his death. Silver Bullet never once left off eating but did offer me one of his tacos. You have to know my assistant to grasp the importance of a gesture like that.

"That makes it more complicated with Valadez," I explained. "Tell him that Cruz is dead. Tell him 'Hernandez is trying to impress his bosses, and you're next on his list.' Ask him for three times as much and make sure he doesn't leave the city."

I didn't have the time, so I was forced to send Silver Bullet to the Buenos Aires garage to ask for next week's payment in advance. (Anyone who knows Kiko will be aware that this is Mission Impossible, so if the boy pulled it off, he would deserve his fifty per cent.) I didn't say a word about the Three Marias because I had no doubt he would ruin the arrangement by accepting all payment in kind. Besides which, I needed to talk to Rosario urgently.

When I left him, he was doing his best to look

like James Bond. Sucking determinedly on his mamey juice through a straw.

*

I like sitting with Rosario at one of the outside tables in a Zona Rosa bar. I can sense how jealous the stupid passers-by are, and see how their rutting wolves' eyes stare at my girl. I like the way she hangs on my arm, laughs out loud, brings her face close to mine and tickles me with her curls. As well as enjoying this for its own sake, it gives me intellectual satisfaction of the Pygmalion kind, because as the weeks go by I can see how she is honing her skills. And I'm the best proof of this there is, because I can't spend five minutes with her before I get an erection. We had a quick drink and finished our conversation in a hotel. What Rosario said left me very confused. My protégée had better information than me on Jones. She and, according to her, all the whores in the Zona Rosa knew that the gringo was making porno movies. He recruited women for fiestas and had a ranch near Hidalgo where he held orgies, to which he invited important personalities. Jones's reputation fluctuated between bad and worse. Apparently, he was a dangerous pervert. Some women who had worked with him disappeared; others turned up dead with signs of torture. Among her acquaintances, Rosario had heard stories of bestial abuse, of floggings, tattoos carved out with knives, rapes with a wide range of objects. In the Zona Rosa none of the women would work with him anymore. They had held meetings and discussed denouncing him to the police, but since nobody ever listens to whores, and seeing that the gringo had powerful friends who were politicians and judges, they decided to let him be, but to protect themselves by warning everyone so that nobody else would fall into his clutches. They considered Jones's death an act of justice. They were pleased that a cockroach like him had been cleared from the streets. Rosario and, in her view, none of the other girls she knew on the game had the slightest idea who could have killed him. She knew the hotel in question and even knew girls who had been there that night, but none of them had seen Jones or the blond man, or had heard anything at all. This might or might not have been true, but they had talked it over and that was that. The only thing certain was that they were all delighted.

I pondered on an intelligence network based on keeping your legs open and your ears pricked, and after experiencing a mixture of humiliation and amazement, I suddenly felt so relieved and happy that, with the money Rosario had given me for her insurance policy – I always tell her: I'm your insurance policy – I took her for a meal and then left her at a cinema with instructions to get more information.

I bought toys and chocolates for the kids, a bottle of Carlos I for myself and a small box for Gloria's earrings. A healthy desire to do nothing crept over me. While I was driving to the Mixcoac apartment I had a brilliant idea: vacations for everyone. I'd book a good hotel for Gloria and the midgets in Acapulco, and offer myself the pleasure of discovering Cancun. One room for me and Lourdes, another for Carlos and Araceli.

Chapter twelve

I woke at nine to a beer and a caress of my head. The caress was ten out of ten, the beer a little colder than I normally like, but I hadn't the heart to tell Gloria that, given the love she was showing me. I know the tricks the female mind can play, but I also know how important it can be for a man – especially if he isn't a hairdresser or a bureaucrat – to get a bit of tenderness first thing in the morning. Malinche must have woken Hernan Cortes in exactly the same way. That's why we're all losers, whether we end up crying under a huge tree like Cortes did, or sitting in the living room glued to the TV.

"Up you get, sleepyhead!" she said with a smile, as though it wasn't her who was waking me up.

"I should be at work by this time," I complained, showing her the alarm clock. "I asked you to wake me at eight."

"I did call you at eight. You answered that only spastics get up early, turned over the other way and carried on snoring."

"This beer is too cold."

"It was better at eight." Gloria wasn't smiling any more.

I drank in silence, pondering on how fickle

women can be. How they can adore the man who loves them, then the next morning treat him like garbage. I watched Gloria coming and going. I know that manoeuvre. Gloria was putting on the performance known as "I at least work". I could feel myself getting annoyed the way I always do when I see a woman feeling so superior because they think the stupidest of tasks is important.

"Do you want something to eat?" she said, as if she were talking to one of her children, as if somehow everything goes better when you eat.

I looked at her patiently. There was no doubt that Gloria was fine to visit once a week.

"I'm going to the hairdresser's today. Would you like me to keep it straight like it is, or should I have a perm?"

"I want it as curly as wool, lots of curls falling into your eyes so I can pull them back and see your face when you're making mad passionate love to me."

"Do you love me?"

"No, I hate you, because you're a cheap whore and have a face like a sick giraffe."

Ah, these indispensable morning bedroom farces. We continued our philosophical debate, lulled by the sound of the vacuum cleaner, until it was half past nine and I decided to get washed and dressed.

As soon as I got out of the bathroom I phoned the office. Maribel wanted to chat, but I didn't. Silver Bullet hadn't arrived yet.

I called the widow's house and the maid from

Oaxaca replied. I would have loved to do my dirty call trick on her. I would have done if Gloria hadn't been around.

"The mistress hasn't got up yet," the maid told me.

"Fine, I'll be straight round," I said. "It's a quarter to ten now. I'll be there at around eleven. Tell your mistress when she wakes up."

"Yes, sir. Atyourservice."

"Are you coming this evening?" Gloria asked, looking the other way as she did so.

"I don't know, woman," I said, stealing up behind her. "I've got a lot of work, and Carlos and Araceli are due back today. I don't know whether I'll be able to come."

I kissed her on the neck. Gloria stiffened and turned her face away. I realized I had hurt her feelings and felt terrible. I had a sudden revelation: the world was a mess; I was a brute to force such a loving good woman to be no more than a mistress to me. I would have kneeled to ask her forgiveness, except that my sense of the ridiculous would not allow me to. I stroked her hair as she tried to pull away. I promised that if Lourdes did not return, nobody would be able to budge me from Mixcoac. I'd make our two families one. I wanted to grow old by her side.

Gloria laughed:

"I want you young," she said. "When you're old I'm going to put you in a home."

She has a sense of humour and what's what, the cow. That's why I love her, among other things.

Seeing I still wasn't dressed, I decided to take her back to bed and make it up to her. Sometimes I wonder what on earth will become of me in ten years' time.

*

"The mistress is not up yet," the maid repeated mechanically. Above and behind her, the curtains twitched at a first floor window. Someone was spying on us. But since the Commander wants the case closed as quickly as possible, I needed to get something out of the widow – she might or might not be the murderer, but she was definitely hiding things. Some of which I already knew about.

The maid from Oaxaca looked at me dismissively. I stood staring up at the window until the curtains opened properly, and I could see Estela Lopez de Jones staring down.

"The mistress has got up," I found myself saying.

And found myself entering the house.

Estela Lopez de Jones was wearing another of her elegant gowns and a discreet amount of make-up. She was polite in the manner of someone who has slept well, is not forced to go out to earn a living, and is receiving a visit from the law, with whom it's never a good idea to fall out.

"If you don't mind, I'll have breakfast while we talk," she said, smiling warmly at me again as if she were my sister rather than an adulterous murderer. "I'm having coffee and cakes. Would you like some, or would you prefer something else?"

I preferred beer, but I accepted coffee.

We made small talk until the breakfast had been served, and the widow had sent the maid off to put a load of washing in the machine.

It was up to me to make the opening move, and since I had no idea what I should or should not mention, I decided to be brutal and reveal that I knew all about the four-handed game of billiards she and her deceased husband used to play with Mr and Mrs Accountant. I soon confirmed that what the accountant had said was true, because in my trade you can tell the answer just by looking at people's faces. I could tell she was hesitating, wondering how much I knew, calculating what she ought to tell me, what she should keep to herself. I knew I was going to be served stuff well past its sell-by date, and that's what I got. Nothing fresh. A crime is a conflict of interests resolved by force, and no one should expect honesty where a conflict of interests is involved. Fortunately for him, Sherlock Holmes could go around with his magnifying glass, spot a mouldy red shirt button and from it deduce that its owner had escaped from a clinic in the East and suffered from dreadful headaches due to a hereditary disease. But, of course, in Mexico Shirley would never even have got a licence, thanks to our laws on the possession and consumption of drugs. Be that as it may, a Mexican policeman at least has the consolation that he is one of the cleanest men in the world. The proof lies in the fact that after he has taken a statement from anyone who is part of a conflict of interests.

the said policeman has to have a bath, so great is the amount of garbage thrown at him.

Estela Lopez de Jones told me about Jones's inclination to betray her with any woman he happened to meet, about the life of a twenty-year-old girl with a drug addict thirty years older than her, of his love affairs with the models he hired. She gave her own version of the explosions, the abuse, the fights, the times Jones treated her in the same way as any of his maids or model-whores, or threatened to throw her out onto the street without a penny, thousands of miles from her home in Bogota. She said the story with the accountant's wife was the last straw, creating a humiliating situation all the time, sometimes even in her own house. It was her story, so she told me how she decided to get revenge in the most obvious way, with the cuckolded accountant himself, someone so dreary that no pleasure, no emotion could possibly contaminate her vengeance. All this drama coincided in Estela's mouth (small and round; selfish and perverse) with slices of toast covered in jam that she had no problem forcing down. She told me – it was her story – about Jones's fury when he discovered her revenge, his shouted threat to kill the accountant and leave her at the first bus terminal. She mentioned secret conversations between the accountant and her dead husband. Then each returned to their original couple. Some time afterwards, Jones organized a kiss-and-make-up party for the four of them. From then on it was pandemonium, everyone and no one in charge, sex swapped and drunken sessions until the early hours. She spoke of her determination to get out, to leave him, to return to Bogota. Of her fears, the cowardice which paralysed her and brought on terrible depression. Of how she had got used to an easy life, her panic at the thought of becoming a shop assistant again, of going back to Colombia a failure, carrying a single suitcase of clothes and having to start from scratch once more.

My head ached from listening to all this. I asked:

"Who brought the drugs?"

"What drugs?" She looked at me warily, halfway through eating a doughnut.

"Cocaine," I said. "The accountant tells a good story too."

Tears trickled down Estela Lopez de Jones's cheeks. I took advantage of the two minutes she spent crying to press my knees against hers under the table. She accepted them, withdrew hers slowly, repeated the same movement a second time. A trickster, a cheat. Carlos Hernandez is a good judge of women.

She used several handkerchiefs to blow her nose then admitted:

"My husband supplied it. There were a lot of drugs in his circle. Jones made all four of us snort it."

"Was that in your orgies?"

"What orgies?" she asked, apparently genuinely surprised that anyone should use such a grandiose term for what went on in their parties. She shook her head at unfortunate memories, lowered her eyelashes to emphasize her embarrassment. She was facing something women always find difficult and unpleasant. (I've known women who have tortured their own children and always, absolutely always, what has been most difficult for them has not been the fact of doing it but having to admit it, to realize other people know it, to feel themselves condemned. Something similar happens with men, of course; perhaps there is a difference in the hypersensitive nature of women, their greater dependence on other people's opinion.) Without looking up at me, she said:

"Yes."

"Did Jones film the orgies?" Now I'd got the word accepted, I wasn't going to let go of it.

"No . . . yes . . . sometimes."

That's the way. My next step would be to ask her to take me to where all this fucking went on; then of course I'd try to get a peek at the films. After that I could suggest we might take our clothes off and reconstruct some of the scenes, the ones with fellatio for example, or with whipped or pene-trated backside. If I guaranteed her protection, perhaps the widow would go for it. The down side was that since in addition to being a widow she was a murderer – a self-made widow, as they call it in Bucareli – she could decide at any moment to get rid of me as well. She might even use the fellatio to bite it off. This thought raced down from my brain to the centre of my body, instantly deflating my jack-in-the-box. If that was the case, I'd better forget about her mouth, stay well away from those piranha teeth of hers. Whatever I did would have to be behind her back, and with her hands in cuffs as well. I imagined the scene and perked up at once.

When the widow had finally finished with her buns and cakes I asked to see the rest of the house. She stood up and led me along corridors that smelled of money, antiquities, signed paintings, plants, pieces of furniture that were new and expensive rather than tasteful, a darkroom whose walls were plastered with photos of attractive young women posing against parks, waterfalls, monuments and ruins. A lot of them were of Estela Lopez de Jones herself: in a bikini by the sea, in a T-shirt and jeans in the garden, in evening gowns and so on. I was able to confirm her appetizing charms and asked if any of the other women was Victoria Ledesma. The widow put on a perfect look of not knowing what I was talking about. We went upstairs, and there it was, together with desks, chests of drawers, mirrors, that round thing women sit on to do their make-up, and a king-size bed large enough to offer more than enough room for four bodies in motion. There was the altar with its huge, plump, welcoming surface. Welcoming yes, because I had come up there to fuck on it, that's what I was there for. Now all I had to do was strip the murderer, use my darting tongue between her legs until she was melting for me, turn her on all fours on top of the tortoise, then position myself behind her so we could make the three-headed monster my fantasy had been sketching ever since the first morning I saw it.

"Nice tortoise," I said, to set the ball rolling.

"A present from my husband," the Aztec virgin replied, strangely serious all of a sudden.

"It's big enough to use as a mattress," I said, giving her one of my looks.

Estela Lopez de Jones turned on her heel and walked out of the room. I was left on my own with the tortoise. I thought of following her and dragging her back by the hair to show her who was boss. To teach her that an Aztec virgin chosen for sacrifice cannot escape her destiny.

A minute later I followed her downstairs. She was sitting in a chair in the living room. The look she gave me showed there had been one of those abrupt role changes that women are so fond of: now she was the Virgin of Guadalupe and I was the ragged beggar Juan Diego. I wasn't going to stand for it. Not me.

"Who was Victoria Ledesma?" I became the grand inquisitor, turning her into one of the witches of Salem.

"Who?"

"Victoria Ledesma."

"I don't know her."

"You should. She worked with your husband on a film about Teotihuacan. A short while later they found her dead body."

"So?"

"Your husband was investigated over her death."
Once again, fear flashed in her eyes, and a
scarcely contained anger.

"I refuse to speak to you any more. Or tell me if
I should have a lawyer to defend myself against a
policeman investigating my husband's death who
treats him more like a criminal than the victim of
a crime."

Like I said: an expert at switching decks. I
wouldn't like to have her as a mistress. I began to
remember a phrase of Schopenhauer's, so I
repeated it:

"You won't need lawyers, if you tell me the
truth. If you lie, you'll definitely need them."

"I don't know anything about that woman. I've
never even heard her name."

A fruitless morning. I was wasting my time, and I
was no longer interested in this tramp with her
outraged expression; I was sick of her.

Before I left I heard that someone had tried to
burgle the house a few days earlier. Apparently a
gang had been doing robberies all over Copilco in
recent weeks. Talking to their neighbours, Estela
and the maid from Oaxaca – who was back from
doing the washing and had joined in our conversation as naturally as if we were three Zapotec
Indians talking about the prices for mats in
Juchitan market – had heard of several break-ins.

The previous Thursday, shortly before two in
the morning, Estela Lopez de Jones had heard
noises at the fence and in the garden. Frightened,
she got out of bed, switched on all the lights on

the top floor and looked out of a window. She shouted for the Indian maid and caught sight of two or three men jumping down into the street from the garden fence. She didn't want to buy a dog, because she was going back to Colombia in a week.

I congratulated her on being so brave, thanked her for all her valuable information and for the two watered-down coffees she had offered me, calculated that in a week the Jones case would be either solved or archived and left, the tortoise having completely slipped from my mind.

Chapter thirteen

I called Lourdes and what I could sense from her voice was a good omen. I know that woman the way you know someone after eighteen years of sharing life's ups and downs with them. We talked about the kids, about work, about the house. I didn't ask her to come back – there was no need, because that's what I had been doing from the moment she crossed the threshold on her way out. I invited her for a coffee that evening, and she accepted. I told her I'd pick her up at seven. We said a fond goodbye.

I dialled the office number and was in luck: Silver Bullet answered the phone. He started speaking, and that was the end of my luck.

"I went to the Buenos Aires," he said. "Everything went fine. But that might be the last time, because they're closing down."

"All right. We'll talk about it later," I replied. I didn't have a lot to say, it's not the sort of thing to talk about, especially given the number of microphones there are waving about everywhere, just waiting to pick up some audible indiscretion.

"I didn't have the same success with the other business," James Bond went on.

"What happened?"

"Nothing. I couldn't find him. I got tired of phoning, so I went to his apartment. He's not there any more. He's gone."

"Who did you talk to?"

"A woman neighbour saw him leaving with two suitcases and getting into a taxi."

"Aha . . . and what about the caretaker?"

"He wasn't there either. I only found two young children. When I questioned them they stated that their mother would be back in half an hour, but I couldn't wait, and the kids didn't know anything anyway."

"OK," I said, and just as I do whenever I say that word, I felt a cretin. "Give me his number and his address."

I called Valadez's apartment. Nobody answered. He'd flown the coop. With my holiday bookings for Cancun.

*

I rang the bell at the Rio Atoyac apartment several times. No reply. A Spaniard with bushy eyebrows came out of the caretaker's cubbyhole. He told me: "Senor Valadez left on a trip yesterday morning." I showed him my credentials and learned that the trip was to Miami and that the declared reason for it was business. Clever son of a bitch! Who could find a democratic Mafioso Cuban in a city where nearly all the foreigners are Mafiosi and democratic! I asked when he would be back, and the Spaniard said: "Senor Valadez will be gone three or four weeks." The apartment was empty, and Senor Olmedo – that was Bushybrows' name – was to collect any mail. That was all. The caretaker did not get mixed up in the lives of people living in the building. He did his job and was paid his wages. He was so full of the importance of his job that I felt like teaching him a lesson or two, but then I thought I might well be back in a month. Not to mention the fact that to a policeman we're all equal before the law, even Spanish caretakers with bushy eyebrows.

A hunch led me to Calle Marsella, between Berlin and Dinamarca Streets, to the first floor of a flashy building where Mr and Mrs Accountant lived. With all my suspects disappearing, my week looked as if it might turn out like the guy's who was hanged on Monday. The cases were different, though. Valadez had reasons to escape and people to escape from. He had to get away from me and Silver Bullet's pressure for payment. With the accountant it was different. In theory, he had merely been one of Jones's victims. There were lots of things to clear up, though. I still had to have a real talk with him, on the understanding that it's the one who controls the money who tends to know the most.

Mr and Mrs Accountant weren't there either.

"They've gone," a neighbour told me. "A removal van came and took all their things."

It's hard not to be in a bad mood when all of a sudden everything turns out badly. I spend the whole day working. I'm given a case in which it's important to keep tabs on various people, and I'm not even assigned an assistant. I have to pay Silver Bullet out of my own pocket. They talk about austerity but put dozens of cops on guard duty for any bureaucratic politician whose number has come up in this presidency.

I asked more questions and learned that the Accountants had gone for good. They had left at the crucial moment, just before I was going to consult Mr Accountant on financial matters. I enquired about removal firms in the area and eventually came up with the man who around two the previous afternoon had taken the Accountants' things to a stall in the La Merced flea market.

"Why to La Merced?" I asked. "He's got more class than that. It would have made more sense to take them to somewhere better."

"He was in a hurry to sell," the van driver explained. "I told him he'd be able to offload them there straightaway, and he accepted the idea."

"Did he know he wouldn't get much of a price?"
"Yes, he knew."

La Merced is full of traders, all kinds of meat, vegetables, fruit, endless disposable objects. Then there are all the old dames of the city who come to buy, a shopping basket on each arm. And there are more whores and pickpockets than there are old women buying all the crap.

When after two hours' search I found the stall, I was confronted by an Arab from Tabasco with the face of an assassin. Once I had shown him my ID and the butt of my gun, he decided to play ball.

He admitted he had le-ga-lly bought a load of furniture from a pale-faced, stupid-looking foreigner. He showed me the receipt : "Received, one million pesos for one load of furniture", signed with a scribble which, he said, was the le-gal signature of paleface.

In La Cotorra they serve the best drinks in the Mexican capital. Generous glasses, more the sort you expect at a friend's house than in a public bar. I sat down to think with a dish of peanuts and a couple of tequilas. The bar was close to where I had to meet Lourdes, and this made the wait more palatable. The Jones case was becoming clearer. There are many reasons for three suspects to disappear on the same day, and none of them is a coincidence. They are all to do with guilt. Those three sons of bitches had done for Jones. The motive had to be money. Which meant that Jones's business – the real, pornographic business – made a healthy profit. And the essential part of any successful business is the market, the customers. Once you have a captive market, which must have been the case here, it's easy to organize the rest. The accountant dealt with all that, the invoices and the clients. So why shouldn't he decide he could take over the business, particularly if a snake like Valadez was tempting him with his contacts, his influence and networks that would mean the two of them could line their pockets with gold? You can get whores just by whistling on any street corner round here, and you can hire someone who can use a camera at the entrance to any TV station. They no longer needed Jones, so between the three of them they got rid of him. Perhaps the man-woman in the hotel was the accountant's wife, using two blond wigs – one for a man, the other for a woman – to conceal her auburn hair and turn the porter's head. Perhaps Mrs Accountant went in disguised as a blonde woman and Mr Accountant came out disguised as a transvestite. She went in with Jones and killed him. He came up the service stairs and joined her. Afterwards, he went out the front way, while she sneaked out of the service exit. Then again, perhaps she went in with Jones and Mr Accountant came in with a local whore, and Valadez arrived with another one. Between them, they dispatched Jones. Mr Accountant dressed up as a transvestite and left. They either drugged the two whores or paid them a good wad of bank-notes, and Valadez left with Mrs Accountant. There were lots of possibilities, and a detective isn't meant to play guessing games. A detective is meant to catch the guilty sons of bitches, give them a thorough interrogation and get at the truth.

I've no idea how many glasses the barman served me, but I know he must have been a magician because all of a sudden he made Madonna appear at my table. I've no idea either why there are times when it's impossible to say "no". And anyway it was already almost eight by now, and it didn't seem a good idea to turn up for Lourdes looking like an advert for Alcoholics Anonymous.

Chapter fourteen

When the taxi travelling along Rio Churubusco crosses La Viga and carries on five hundred yards towards the airport, two dark-coloured cars without licence plates appear, block its path, and force it to a halt. Four men armed with submachine guns and sawn-off shotguns leap out of the cars. They pull Valadez out of the backseat, throw him into one of the cars and speed off. The taxi driver is a statue nobody wastes any time on.

At six that evening, the accountant and his wife return to their hotel with airline tickets for the night flight to Miami. They go into Room 402, and Mr Accountant comments: "Well, that's the end of that." When they hear this the two men hiding in the bathroom grin at each other. Then they burst into the bedroom. They are carrying pistols with silencers.

Chapter fifteen

Presenting Beauty to the Beast, I explained to Rosario's younger sister that for the rest of the day she would be Esmeralda like in the novel, and that my friend had a beautiful spirit. There was nothing untrue in what I said, and the girl's silence showed how intelligent she was. Her job was to keep the monster happy. Lobster, squid, maguey worms or whatever else he might fancy to eat, the best alcohol and a honeymoon worthy of the Virgin Mary. In other words, whatever he asked for and was up to. "Be a guiding star for him." Carlos Hernandez knows how to look after his friends, and what that guy had just given him was priceless.

It's true that the information was common knowledge among the whores of the Zona Rosa, but now – the most important thing! – the police had got wind of it too. Once upon a time there was a ranch, bought in the name of a gentleman from Los Angeles, whose owner had never been traced. The police searched for his whereabouts for a whole month before giving up. The case was so cold it might almost be called frozen, like the beers my women offer me when they forget to bring them warm, and yet those in charge of it – "I can't say a word about any of this," Quasimodo dixit, with a wonderful grin on his lopsided mouth – had evidence that Jones frequently went there, and that every fortnight there would be huge celebrations. Limos, celebrities, females like luxury felines. They would start arriving on the Saturday morning and leave late on Sunday.

Parties, drugs, pornography: Jones. A well-signposted road. Situations that led to – and here was the mystery – an exit in the bullet hole in the back of the gringo's head.

Rosario had told me about the ranch. But now I knew its name and location: a turning off the road to Hidalgo, beyond a rustic wooden arch proclaiming "Rancho El Porvenir". Which in Jones's case might just as well have read "The Worms".

Quasimodo could not tell me anything because it was not me who was investigating Victoria Ledesma's death, and since it was being dealt with by another police force I could not get a search warrant which would allow me to raid "El Porvenir". In any case, it had already been searched by our police colleagues. Not forgetting the fact that there are useless and blind people – as well as blind people who don't want to see – the whole world over.

I needed help to get anywhere, so I went to see the Commander. His opening salvo was to tell me that Valadez was dead, riddled with bullets and dumped at the side of a road, and that Mr and Mrs Accountant were also dead, murdered in their hotel room with shots to the body and head. You need to know the Commander to realize that this news was much more important for my relation to him than for anything to do with the Jones case. I was the slave, he the master – Hernandez-knownothing versus Commanderknowall, Subordinateuseless versus Commanderuseful – showing yet again my inability to find out something which, since I was in charge of the case, I ought to know about better than anyone. The fact that it was he who – sitting comfortably in his chair – could give me the news proved various things, all of them essential: 1) he was the one who had the information and the power; 2) without him I was nobody; 3) therefore it would be best for me to devote the rest of my life to making sure he got his kickbacks; 4) if I did that, he could perhaps bring himself to excuse such monumental slackness; 5) would to God that I could understand some day that the individual is nothing, it's the institution that is everything. This last point had an equally essential corollary: it was true in my case, in that of Hernandezmisternocount, but not in his, that of Commandermisterbigboss. I smoked my way through an entire cigarette while I deduced all this.

When he heard my news the Commander looked at me strangely and wanted to know who my sources were. I told him about Estela Lopez de Jones, the accountant and Valadez, and though his poker-face did not slip once, something in the effort he was making to stay calm told me I was entering forbidden territory. When I asked for permission to search the ranch he gave so many excuses, raised so many problems of jurisdiction and proper authority, who was responsible and other kinds of crap, that the only thing I understood was that he didn't want to see me there. I would have to act on my own.

The case was beginning to interest me.

Paying a visit to the ranch secretly all alone one night, going inside with a revolver in my right hand and in the other a dim torch (that's what they always call them in novels, though to me the word says more about the people carrying them) and exposing myself to getting my very own bullet-hole in the head is what cops do in all the films. What Hernandez did was call Quasimodo and tell him my boss did not seem interested in me nosing round the ranch. Perhaps because his vital juices had all been poured out as libations on erotic altars, my friend was very cautious. "If there's money involved, there's danger too." And he gave his judgement: "Being a poor cop is better than having two quarts of mud in your lungs." He was right, but so was I. In my defence, I quoted the example of Christopher Columbus, who, if he had been put off by the legends of sea serpents that devoured ships, of the children of darkness lying in wait for him in the *Mare Tenebrosum*, would have stayed in Madrid playing dominoes and drinking a brandy chaser in his local inn, and nobody would be celebrating him or accusing him of genocide five hundred years after his adventure.

In the end I managed to convince him. The only drawback was that he didn't have any jurisdiction or authority to get into the ranch either. He was just the man who ran the Archive. Besides which, he had hardly slept, and was still recovering from the mystic powers of the gypsy Esmeralda. He did, though, know one of the cops investigating Victoria Ledesma's death, an individual by the name of Arganaraz, who, if there was money in it, would be more than happy to collaborate in the undertaking and earn himself a third of any profits. I had been thinking of keeping seventy per cent for myself and giving thirty to Quasimodo, so such a sudden reduction in my percentage took the wind from my sails. I looked on the bright side when I considered that the protection money I got from Kiko and my protégée was barely enough to keep me in cigarettes, whereas even a third of such a big deal could mean I was no longer poor.

The next day we had breakfast and swapped card collections. Arganaraz said everyone in the police knew about Jones's pornography racket, that there was a film everybody had seen, although no one knew what had become of it, in which a whore played Snow White, and the dwarves had done everything apart from fuck her in the eye sockets, that the case had got nowhere because the gringo was protected from high up, the big chiefs, his embassy, and who knows where else. Short-arsed and skinny, a typical Mexican "race of bronze" type, Arganaraz looked so greasy and slippery he could have been in one of those Hollywood films where the Mexicans are always the double-crossers. I told him my theories about the blond assassin, and he doubled up laughing. He and his colleagues had already solved the case. Jones had got above himself and tried to blackmail someone he shouldn't have. "An untouchable, get it?" He lost out, of course. "You can't beat an untouchable." Legally, there was nothing to be done. But whoever found the video-cassettes was onto a fortune. They had searched the ranch until they were tired of it. It was full of French champagne and other imported liquor, which strangely vanished in the course of the investigation; there were immense round beds; waterbeds and others that moved up and down, ideal for fat slugs or those afraid of a heart attack; opposite the largest bed there was a two-way mirror, one of those you can see through from behind and film without being seen. To complete the picture there were all the usual accoutrements in places like these: porno magazines and films, rubber dildos, whips, handcuffs, black leather jackets with metal spikes, everything you could imagine. Regular visitors included important politicians and police chiefs, ambassadors, men and women who spoke English. By sheer chance no one had seen the Pope there. As I listened to him, I was thinking how people find it necessary to exaggerate: no one can describe how they had a coffee without embroidering the story. But even allowing for this, what was left sounded juicy enough, and exactly what I had been expecting.

"The caretaker knows me and will let me in," Arganaraz added.

"Fine, but what are we looking for?" Quasimodo looked at us as though we were behaving oddly, as if we were drunk and forcing him to stay sober. "If they've searched the place and taken everything away, what exactly are we after?"

I seized the opportunity to put Mr Race of Bronze in his place.

"Jones was killed, and it can't have been for his failings as a host," I said. "It's possible the gringo made a habit of blackmailing his friends, filming them from behind the mirror in not very saintly positions, and that's why he ended up with a hole in his head. We don't know, sweetheart. It's my hunch. But just imagine I'm right. If it is, what we're looking for is a secret hiding-place where he kept the photos and films. If we find nothing, it's simply another day wasted. Like all those we spend snoozing in a bar or in the office. And if we find something, we're made. By the way," I said, addressing Arganaraz this time, "is the place behind the mirror concealed or visible?"

"Concealed." When someone with a double-crosser's face smiles, it only makes it worse. "It's a tiny room about five-feet square that you get into via a wardrobe."

"That fits," I said.

We chatted for a while about the risks of being a blackmailer, the importance of bearing in mind what had happened to the gringo, the accountant and his wife and Valadez, and we agreed if we

110

found any stuff we would take into account both the dangers and the possible price tag. We also tried to shake Quasimodo out of his gloomy mood and make him feel more optimistic about the adventure. "Running an archive means you classify information and draw realistic conclusions from it. Nothing good will come of this for us," he said. I realized that if we put things off for too long, Quasimodo would find an excuse to back out. So I insisted there was no time like the present, and that a man of action doesn't spend his life mulling over everything but leaps in and gets what he wants out of it. Arganaraz agreed with everything and was even more enthusiastic than me, talking about the fortune waiting somewhere for those brave enough to grab it, plus other nonsense you only ever hear on TV, and although his treacherous face still worried me, for the moment I needed him on my side. Quasimodo kept silent, a silence so deep that even without looking at him you could see his scepticism and understand that the habit of spending his life shut up in an archive had, begging his pardon, softened his brain.

We drank a tequila to help settle our breakfast and set off for the ranch.

Chapter sixteen

A few miles before we reached our destination, someone started shooting at us. They were hunting us down from a wood to the left of the road. It was a well-chosen spot, far enough away from the ranch to avoid any relation to it, so that the headlines in the morning newspapers could report our deaths without any link there. For example, "Three policemen die in hail of bullets on side-road." Or one of us at least, because I was hit in the head and can't believe I'm still alive. We pulled up on the right and returned their fire flat out on the ground behind the car. Our revolvers were useless at that range, and the bastards took advantage to shoot out all the windows of the Atlantic. (More work for Kiko.) We could hear them laughing and shouting: "You'd better turn back, assholes. We're going to finish you off. You've really messed up this time." And more words we didn't catch, because we were busy putting as much distance as possible between us and the source of the shouting and the gunfire. This went on for some time, with them firing and us crawling away as fast as we could, until we came to a gully and threw ourselves down it, commenting on what had happened to us. "We're fucked." "They were lying in wait for us." "Great idea of yours, Carlitos." "So great they tried to kill us." "Not to kill us, just scare us off."

All of a sudden our debate was interrupted by the explosion of three grenades and flames rising from what once had been my faithful Atlantic. After that we heard the sound of cars racing away. We decided they had all gone, but that it would be better not to try to find out if they'd left anyone behind to check our movements.

"Well, that's the end of that adventure," said the ugliest man in the world.

"It's not over yet," I replied.

"If we're going to get killed," insisted Quasimodo, with the same reluctance he had shown all morning, "we ought at least to know why. But we don't even know what we're looking for. We're playing stupid blind man's bluff. If either of you is interested, that's quite enough for me."

Despite the hammer-blow to the back of my head, I was still lucid and determined that reality should confirm my analysis.

"Look," I said. "Edgar Hoover, the big chief of the FBI, ruthless persecutor of communists, blacks and Jews, homophobic guardian of Calvinist morality, the archetypal Wasp, was a homosexual. And if someone like him could destroy a myth like that, I'm willing to accept any transgression, whoever may be doing it."

"What are you talking about, Carlitos?" Quasimodo was looking at me in exactly the same way

Lourdes does when she thinks I'm lying or doesn't believe a word.

"What's a Wasp?" Arganaraz asked, showing his education.

"A Wasp is a White Anglo-Saxon Protestant: the cream of gringo society. Such superior people they're even more high-class than Nazis. I'm talking about people we don't know who they are exactly, but we do know that nobody takes part in an orgy to be on their best behaviour: for that it'd be better to stay at home and perhaps get lucky with your wife. So I wouldn't be surprised if in "El Porvenir" we find pictures of some honourable autocrat from one of our sacred institutions busy sucking the dick of a Senegalese sailor."

Quasimodo produced a hipflask lined in green leather and full of rum. Arganaraz handed round unfiltered Pall Malls and sat down against a tree. We did the same, as there's nothing better than feeling comfortable to help recapitulate. Someone didn't want us poking around the ranch. The place had already been turned over without anyone finding the film of the president and the Senegalese sailor. But if there was nothing there, why didn't they want us in the ranch? Because someone knew the film existed and didn't like the idea of us finding it. They must be priceless images that would soon find a buyer. It was our business to find them. Someone wanted us dead. That was the risk. Too big a risk.

"Let's get this straight." Despite the sensation that I had a dagger plunged into my neck, I tried to be clear. "We're real cops, not like the ones on TV. We do a job where we could be chopped to pieces any day. Our wages are enough to rent a cave in Nezahualcoyotl and buy a Beetle to pay off in twelve years, if we starve our families in the meantime. Why do we do it, rather than opening a café near a ministry or a contraband stall in Tepito? Is it because we believe in our mission, in the vocation of serving the public, of being the custodians of the law and justice?"

"Don't de daft, Carlitos."

"We get things out of it too."

"I'm coming to that. I knew colleagues who found themselves appointed as customs officers on the northern border. Within a year they'd bought houses, cars even for their pet dogs, time-shares on the beach. They changed beyond rec-ognition. A year later they were all dead, because there's hot competition for jobs like that. But nobody took a peso from their families. Each to his own, and whoever gets the chance has to take it."

"I'm not interested in being a corpse weighed down with gold."

"And I don't want to have to die so the parasites in my family can visit Paris."

"I also know of people who struck it rich and then vanished. Nobody thought of killing them, because they were in another country. What I'm trying to say, and tell me if I'm wrong, is that we put up with all the shit because we're sure that one day we'll get lucky, and it will change into honey and champagne. The chance arises, and if you're in the right place at the right time, you grab it. Yes or no?"

I could see them wavering, as fear and greed fought it out inside them. I was scared too. Scared for Lourdes, Gloria, for my kids and for myself. But if all three of us were scared, we'd never do anything. So in my capacity as ringleader I had to conceal my fear and prevent them from seeing the shortcomings in my plan.

"They already know we're here," Quasimodo said, lighting another cigarette. "We'd need time to search the ranch, and in that time they could come back and finish us off."

"I could put my gun to the caretaker's head and give him ten seconds to spill the beans." Arganaraz drank the last of the rum and licked the hipflask.

"What if he doesn't? We don't even have an hour to put the fear of God into him properly."

I don't know why I say certain things. I'd like to be at home, with a couple of beers just the right temperature, a salami pizza and a good film to watch on the video. I sincerely think that if we go on with this comic strip we're aiming headfirst for disaster, and I'm willing to swear that a low-ranking cop can only get somewhere if he tags along with his bosses. If it were otherwise, the world would be incomprehensible, and we'd all be in anarchy. What I need is something to relax me, a session with the Three Marias, three tongues slowly travelling up and down every inch of my body, or to get Lourdes and Gloria drunk and take them both to bed, or to lie in the sun getting a good tan and sniffing the salt sea air in Cancun. Anything not to be lying here in a gully with a bit of lead in the back of my neck, talking to a couple of losers about our chances of defying the rich and powerful and becoming millionaires. All of which means I've really no idea what made me say to them:

"I've got a better idea."

". . ."

"We don't know what there is or where it is, but we know someone who does."

Arganaraz, a clumsy double-crosser with a sneaky cowardly character, was torn between the dream of getting rich and panic at losing everything. Quasimodo was a different matter. An intelligent and wary bird, he had signed up for the ride because things looked good to start with, or perhaps because he felt he still owed me a favour. But both of them gave me a chance, both wanted to know what I meant.

"My Commander knows," I said.

"What's the plan, Carlitos?"

Chapter seventeen

It took me an hour to convince my colleagues of the merits of my plan: merits which, if the truth were told, I was not convinced of myself. Night was falling by the time I called the Commander.

If Plan A failed, I offered a Plan B, and it was this that persuaded Quasimodo and Arganaraz not to abandon me. When I stood up I felt dizzy. I needed to find a pharmacy and get some painkillers that would calm the throbbing discomfort in my neck. It must have been due to all the effort I had to make to overcome two people obstinately resisting me. I did it by showing them that we were already done for. "They know who we are, and they can finish us off whenever they want to." At the same time, I tried to get into their thick skulls the idea that the music was still playing, so we had to go on dancing. "If we succeed, each of us comes out looking like Pedro Infante; if things don't go so well, we turn to Plan B; and if everything is a disaster – and we'd have to be really unlucky for that to happen – we hide for a while, make use of our holidays to get new documents then we hold up a provincial bank and leave the country." It was when they said "fine" that I stood up and almost fell over.

I asked them how my head looked, and they told me I'd been hit, as if I didn't know. I wanted to see my car one last time, to say goodbye to my Atlantic. A car may be just a chunk of metal, but then again a house is nothing more than bricks and cement. It's what we put into them that makes them important. Chunks of our lives, our memories. It didn't seem right to walk away without having a last look. I wouldn't leave a dying dog – I wouldn't even leave Arganaraz to bleed to death. Perhaps it was just the pain in my head. Climbing the gully felt like it might be the last task I was asked to perform in this world. We had to do it anyway to get back on the road and walk back to the city. I was thinking of my family as I scrambled up. I couldn't see anything except for a red mist in front of my eyes. I had to get my family out of harm's way. As soon as I got to a phone I'd send Carlos and Araceli to stay with their mother. Nobody in my office or elsewhere in the police knew about Gloria's apartment (at least, so I hoped), so I could hide there if necessary. When we got to the top of the gully – with me hanging on to the arms of my two colleagues, whose heads weren't filled with lead – and reached the Atlantic, I became even more determined. They were going to pay for this. I'd put a bullet in each knee of every one of the sons of bitches who had destroyed my car. I was quite calm. I've known guys who've had a bullet enter the back of their head and come out through the mouth, and all that happened was they lost a couple of teeth, and others who only realized years later they had a piece of lead in their top storey.

It's only natural that at first you feel a bit giddy, and things look rather blurred. But I didn't need glasses to see as clear as day that more than one donkey with stripes on his arm seemed to think Carlos Hernandez had been put on this earth with the sole purpose of making their lives more comfortable and profitable. When they gave out tickets for this world, Hernandez was given second class, standing room only, the bleachers. And he was meant to be grateful he didn't get one of the tickets reserved for Indians, dogs, blacks, or women. (Even though the proper way to remember Baudelaire is with a good few drinks inside you, it's not bad to do it with a bullet in the head either.) They even allowed him to go to university so he could get an education and be more useful to them. Their faces. He'd just love to see their faces when he put a bullet in their knees.

Then again, three cops without a car between them aren't much of a threat to anyone, especially on a side-road somewhere near Hidalgo. I saw some animals in the distance and think I may even have suggested that if it came to it we could ride them to the main road and try to get help or steal a car.

"We'll have to walk," Arganaraz said, and just hearing him exhausted me so much I had to lie down.

I remembered a dream I had had a few days earlier and stared up at the sky to see if the buzzards or crows were coming for me. The sky was a red sea, so the only birds in it must have been flamingos or parrots.

I was willing to do anything, so long as I did not have to get up, so I sent them off to the main road to find a car. "Don't move," they told me, which threatened to make me laugh so much it made my ribs ache just thinking about it. I laid my head on the ground and stayed like that until I heard the insistent sound of a horn. I sat up and dedicated a loving smile to Lourdes, who was bringing me my beer, except that it wasn't Lourdes but a red Beetle, driven by a red terrified woman driver. Quasimodo and the other guy had turned red too. If Manitu had been there as well we could have had a nice game of dominoes. And if Lenin had happened along, we could have made up a basketball team and called ourselves the "Hidalgo Reds" or something similar.

I crawled over to the Beetle and sat in the back. To show my sense of humour I cracked a joke. "Kill the granny," I said, and the red lady started to cry. "'She knows too much," I went on, and she started swearing that never for any reason in her whole life would she say a word to anyone. "You're a gossipy old cow," I explained. "As soon as we let you go you'll run around telling everyone about the great adventure you've had. So you can die now or be abused in ways you've never even imagined. Which is it to be?" The truth is I was talking simply not to faint again – and to have a bit of fun as well. I was dying, and I didn't want them all to see it. "My last wish is for you to suck my dick," I told her, making her sob even more loudly. "Drop her off," I ordered the others. They stopped the car, and the old dear scuttled off. To give the game away to the first asshole she met.

My men were talking things over. I pretended to be asleep and listened to what they were saying. They both thought I had suffered concussion, that the blow to my head had knocked me witless, and that there was nothing to be done with me. Above all, it was impossible to storm the Commander's house and persuade him to tell us who had been doing what to whom (man to man, because if it had been a woman, there wouldn't be such a fuss) in the film or photo everyone was looking for, or to show him it would be better for him to talk than to find himself dead in the line of duty, with his family raped and murdered and his house consumed by flames. It wouldn't even be possible to try Plan B, which consisted of burgling our host's place, taking all his jewels, silverware and cash, and taking the Commander and all his credit cards along with us to get more cash out of the machines.

"Carlitos is done for," Quasimodo complained.

"I'm out of here, Rivas," said Arganaraz, showing just what a creep he was, because no one even halfway decent calls Quasimodo by his real name. Not to mention the bad luck it brings – one of the few times he's been called that was the day before the '85 earthquake.

"As soon as we get to the city, I'm off. Maybe no one saw me or even knows I was in the car. If I stay with this lunatic any longer I'll wake up in the morgue tomorrow."

"You're dead already, Arganaraz. Both of you are." I came round again and for the fourth time gave them my clinching argument. "The only chance you have of avoiding it is by sticking with me."

This led to a long, tedious discussion revolving around children, the future, madness and what is or is not possible. What most impressed me was the way people can change, because neither of them was bright red anymore: they were both a sort of misty pink verging on deathly grey, which, thinking back, I should perhaps have seen as a bad sign. I eventually won out by employing a trick that works every time. When others are floundering in uncertainty, you have to seem completely sure of yourself. That makes you the person who knows what's going on, whereas their doubts show their ignorance.

"Let me give him a call, then we'll decide," I told them. They agreed, so I got out and rang the Commander at home.

*

I adopted a tone somewhere between professional eagerness and sheer excitement:

"I've got important news on the gringo case, boss. There are some delicate matters I need to

123

talk to you about. I can't sort them out on my own, or discuss them on the phone."

Nine o'clock at night. A good time to invade a house and turn into a burglar.

"Come and see me," said the Commander.

"Let's go and talk to him, then afterwards we'll decide," I told my companions, so they would realize there was no going back.

"Look," I said. "It was that old bastard who had us shot at. If things go badly, we finish him off ourselves, then home to bed." (Obviously I was planning to go into hiding, and would tell Quasimodo to do the same.) "Tomorrow we show up for work as usual, and that's that. No one will link us to an armed burglary. There are gangs holding up families in their homes every night. In fact, there's one operating right now in Copilco, and the Commander lives quite near there.

"He lives in San Angel, and that's nowhere near." Arganaraz, as argumentative as ever.

We were soon at the house. I presented myself on the interphone, and the door opened. Two minutes later I'd got my gun out and was holding it to the head of my boss, a man apparently unable to believe what was happening to him. Quasimodo and Arganaraz looked even more surprised than him, and the one who looked most surprised of all must have been me. No chance. This must be how things look when you jump out of a plane several thousand feet in the air and go into freefall without opening the parachute, because you know it's there and because you want to enjoy the sense of adventure and terror for as long as they last.

This purple-faced man, with matching purple furniture, was stammering as he peered down the barrel of my gun. He was trembling faced by his inferior, Carlos Hernandez, Hernandezatyour-service, someone he thought he could count on who never seemed dangerous because his job was to say "Yes, boss" in the same way that this bastard stammered "Yes, boss" whenever he talked to a superior. All of which happened in the real world but did not have to happen when reality turns into a nightmare. That man feared Carlos Hernandez because Carlos Hernandez had just ushered in chaos.

Sacred and cursed as only murderers and saints can be, Carlos Hernandez renounces nor-mality and boredom, renounces TV and speeches, watches and calendars, rejects the idea of doing today what he did yesterday, refuses to look at the present with the eyes of the past, thumbs his nose at regulations and codes of behaviour in the DO and all the rest of the motherfucking police, forgets all his routines, casts off his lethargy, will not comb his hair or shave, tells his neighbours what he thinks of them whenever he meets them, and when meet-ing certain women neighbours caresses breasts and hips, laughs at the newspaper headlines, shows his collection of condoms to primary school teachers, suggests sex on the spot with young ladies selling religious tracts, believes that anyone who doesn't lend a book is a numbskull, and anyone who doesn't give it back is even more stupid, will never again say "at your service", much less "at your orders". A friend only to cats and drunks, condemned men and stray dogs, whores and homosexuals, communists and human rights defenders, guerrilleros and feminists, pariahs and gunmen, smokers and liberation theologists, an admirer of Zapata and Pancho Villa, but of no one who wears a suit and tie and carries a briefcase, scornful of Sanborns, postmodernism, the President's opinions and Hollywood films, bored by men of maize and the idea of Mexico "race of bronze", tired, overwhelmingly weary of being a policeman ... Carlos Hernandez watches incredulously as the colours in the room swing towards blue, thinks it must be because night has fallen: all he knows is he enjoys feeling that the Commander is afraid of him.

That was all. I could kill him, and I was off my head – because you had to be crazy to force your way into his house, threaten him with a gun and demand he hand over a photo showing the Chief of Police fornicating with an iguana. And since I was lost to this world anyway, it was increasingly likely I might get it into my head to pull the trigger. I was the problem. Arganaraz – a loser who was going to betray me at the first opportunity – and Quasimodo – lost in his Archive, slave to an old debt – were simply obeying a superior will, a clearer vision, you might say, if it weren't for that fact that I was seeing everything a very Proustian shade of turquoise at that precise moment. I decided for them. I freed them from the problem of having to think. Although perhaps they were regretting having a leader with a bullet in his skull that made him confuse lettuces with orchids and who seemed determined to lead them straight to prison or death.

I'm surrounded by people of little faith. People incapable of knowing what they want, and if by chance they do stumble on the answer, too scared to say "I want this". I know them well, because I used to be one of them. Perhaps you need to have been shot in the back of the head and to have had your third eye opened to be able to see, I mean to really see, without pay-cheques and school fees, without nine-to-five and Christmas holidays, without all the smokescreen we've had injected into our veins, without what we are not, and are not even interested in, preventing us from remembering the only true being we have ever been: the magical shadow of what was once a child. The child who imagined the impossible and hoped to grow up to achieve it. The same being I am now, restored thanks to a hole in the head, with the eyes of a reptile that can see the world is green, someone determined to recover what all those who have fed off my flesh and my life have stripped me of: the Commander, Lourdes, Gloria, my children, the shopkeepers of this city, the banks, the teachers, my colleagues at work, all those who were close to me and banded together to turn me into a donkey and then all lined up to jab the donkey with a cattle-prod. All those who said: "Work, Carlos, bend your back, grind your bones, earn money, I expect it of you because I'm your boss, it's your duty because I'm your wife, you can't abandon us because we're your children, you have to watch over us because we're inhabitants of this city, you have to have your papers in order, you have to make your payments on the money you've borrowed, take out insurance, pay for your own funeral, don't stop and rest, Carlos, you've got to go on working." Let's be clear about it: not even those who most cared for me or loved me, not one of them was ever capable of saying: "Have your cake and eat it, live it up, bet all your money, the world is covered in a cloud of stupidity and resignation, don't breathe it in, be yourself, set off for Abyssinia, be like the bird and the tiger, don't just die underneath your TV dinner tray, don't die either in your office or at home, and don't let the tears of women stop you, there are other women and other parties to go to, there are seas to cross, adventures to live. They've robbed you of everything, Carlos: look at your grey face, your yellow teeth, your wrinkles, your shifty eyes, take a good look at your frozen bones, how death is rising through your flogged animal's flesh, look how you're dying on your feet, Carlos Hernandez. Get on with it."

The Commander said something. His lips moved, but I couldn't catch the words. Arganaraz and Quasimodo grabbed me from behind and took away my gun. Everything went black. It's harder to die than to live.

Chapter eighteen

Bingo. Full house. Case closed. The murderers showed they had the kind of intelligence and skill that could leave all clues at a dead end. Anyone who can do that, whatever his motives or aims, is bound to create a state of affairs which for the average Mexican policeman (or the police of any other country) will be as indecipherable as classical Arabic and will end up with him collapsing in the first bar he comes across, anywhere he can drown his despair and bewilderment in tequila. Someone always appears to knock over the amateurs' chips and make crime what it should be: a game for professionals, people who, thanks to their lengthy experience, their local knowledge and the means they have at their disposal, are the only ones who can see things through to the end, even an investigation. Science, in other words. And wielding power.

Jones – sadistic pornography – money. Mr and Mrs Accountant see the opportunity and recruit Valadez to do the deed. On the night of the crime Mrs Accountant goes out with Jones. She hides her auburn hair under a blonde wig. She's done her make-up differently. "Today I want to be a new woman for you. I want you to make love to me as if we had just met, as if you had just picked me up in the street." That's what she says to him, or some other similar nonsense. Pornophiles like games of that sort. All men do, in fact. Which, following strict Aristotelian logic, must mean that all men are pornophiles. Mr Accountant or Valadez, or both of them, follow her to the hotel where she goes with Jones. Mrs Accountant kills him, wipes off her make-up, changes her wig for a man's. Leaving the hotel, she speaks in a gruff voice, makes her gestures and gait more masculine. She puts on an act, and convinces the hotel porter she's a transvestite. Two hundred yards from the hotel, she gets into a waiting car. An auburn-headed woman pretending to be a blonde who turns into a fair-haired man. Too much.

Quasimodo looks at me sadly, and I discover that sadness goes hand-in-hand with ugliness. The least sadness in the world must be Kim Basinger's, because she is so beautiful even when she cries. Kim-smile, Kim-glasses, Kim-tears are simply different versions of her lips, her eyes, her skin. But the sadness of an ugly person is pathetic because it's so pure. Which explains the success of Frankenstein, Quasimodo (Victor Hugo's) and all the other "good" monsters. They convince us by being both ugly and sad. Their ugliness simply becomes part of their sadness, adding to it and increasing its intensity.

"You looked so out of it, I decided to help you, Carlitos," he tells me. "Even against your will, and knowing you wouldn't like it."

I feel like kicking his head in. But I need him to finally resolve a case I have to close. I've got this evening and tonight to find the proof. Tomorrow, even though Jones, Victoria Ledesma, Valadez and Mr and Mrs Accountant will still have open files, they will disappear into the silent stacks of the archives, carefully classified and labelled, where they'll sleep the endless winter of those who simply appear as a record of the facts, memory and, occasionally, as a launching pad for possible future vindication.

The first thing is to get my hands on some beer. They kept me prisoner in a clinic for three days, feeding me injections and food for sick people. A white ghostly place filled with sexless nurses, as bad tempered as old maids and programmed not to give any information to their victims. I had never been in that penitentiary before, and hope never to be there again. They kept me on fruit juice and pap for three days, as if I were a baby rather than a hardened criminal.

I'm thrilled to see that Quasimodo has regained his normal rat-grey colour and that the air and sky have gone back to their usual soot and ozone. I'm even more thrilled to have left that secret clinic where I was afraid that any of the injections they gave me might send me to sleep forever. The robotic nurses who were in charge of my body – not so much as a finger touching me that suggested anything personal, much less female – aroused such a powerful nostalgia in me for the caresses of Lourdes, Gloria and Rosario that if any of them gets wind of it, they can start choosing the colour of the noose to put around my neck right now. I was thinking the whole time that the satanic Doctor No or Mengele would look in on me and decide that the moment had come to neutralize me. I suppose I've been lucky, and I'm pleased to be breathing in three hundred parts per million of polluted air while I savour a beer that would be perfect if it had been left to chill only three minutes longer.

I explain to Quasimodo that I care about my friends, and that's the only reason why I haven't sent him to the cemetery. I know no one is perfect, and I don't think I'm in any position to go around judging my neighbour. If he ran out, abandoning me in my hour of greatest need, and if he thought that his betrayal was for my own good, so be it. I'm not one to split hairs or to call into question other people's word of honour. All I want to get clear is that I can decide for myself what suits me. It's for me to say what it is in my best interest. I've got a mouth, and when I need help I'll shout for it. Although I can't imagine myself asking to be disarmed so that my chief enemy can toss my bones into a dungeon.

Quasimodo looks so sad that even for me his ugliness becomes unbearable. And since I can't bear to see a monster cry, I continue to reassure him that we're talking among friends, and that Arganaraz is a completely different matter – laying aside the fact that it was Quasimodo who brought him along unasked – because Arganaraz is not only not my friend but is a first-class bastard, a rogue who sells his sisters as whores, a spider who should be crushed: something I'll be happy to do as soon as I lay my eyes on his cheating face.

We knock back four beers in La Cotorra, and I tell him of my plan. He hesitates, considers my concussion and the possibility that I am permanently deranged. I can see he is in the grip of a desperate struggle between feelings of loyalty and guilt (at having failed me when I needed him) and the certainty that this new adventure is even crazier than all those that have gone before, and that Carlitos seems determined to lead him to prison or death.

Things get more complicated still when I notice that one of the Mengele nurses is sitting at a nearby table, observing me and shaking her head.

No chance. We are what we are. We drink a few tequilas to settle our stomachs, to get rid of that bloated feeling a gut full of beer gives, then I push Quasimodo into the car, and we head for the house in Copilco.

"This makes us quits. This is the last time I'll listen to you, Carlitos," he says wearily.

I let it drop. I don't give him the reply he deserves. Being sensitive gets you nowhere, and I need him to help me raid Estela Lopez de Jones's house, wring a confession out of her and find proof.

I know she didn't kill Victoria Ledesma, or Jones, or Mr and Mrs Accountant, or Valadez. She was simply in the eye of all the storms. Nobody can

134

accuse her of anything, there's no clause in the penal codes that condemns opportunism by someone who adds to all the filth but does not get their own hands dirty, someone who tolerates things with a smile, who subtly makes things worse when they speak. I know her style. I can see her wiping away a tear in honour of the person who built up a pile of money for her and heaving a sigh at the thought of the other, already deceased acquaintances. Calm, serene and dignified after the tears. Catwoman at the banquet. Owner of a large share of the business. A retired millionairess-assistant in a cheap clothes store who will now be able to live off her investments for the rest of her life. Or so she thinks. And if I know all this, it's because there's no one else left. Just her and the people who ordered the death of three kamikazes threatening the bureaucratic dream in the Jones case. If I know this, it's because there's money in it. I know what's going on, so I can see that, for now at least, Estela Lopez de Jones is the key to unravelling a story of filthy money and violence.

We reach the place. Everything is as it should be. Which would be terrible if it weren't so comprehensible. The Oaxacan maid comes to the door as usual, asks "Who is it?" and lets us in. Her mistress appears, charming and friendly, not in the least bit surprised. When she sees me there's no nervous outburst; she doesn't fling herself on the floor to confess. What the lady of the house does is offer us coffee. She doesn't fling herself on me clutching a kitchen knife, or even kneel down to stick her face between my legs.

I make the first move. I tell her what I'm looking for and see her become wary. Quasimodo follows the instructions I gave him. His role is not to talk but to show the lady a perverse, repugnant incubus ready and willing to unleash more sexual sadism on her body than that shown by her husband in ten thousand feet of film. The beast looks at her lasciviously, rolling his obscene yellow eyes as he studies the face, mouth, neck, breasts, stomach and legs not only of our anxious hostess but of the terrified Oaxacan maid too. His tongue traces lewd graffiti on his mandrill's snout. One paw fondles his testicles, monstrously huge and abominably shaped in their imagination. Impossible to turn back now. I have to go on with the farce until we uncover fear, because it's in the magic of fear that the truth is revealed. The maid is peering at us from the kitchen, probably wondering whether she should call the police, and what she could say about a perverse policeman who, apart from having to put up with the most ghastly face handed out by the Devil, has done nothing to anybody, and who, even though he is stroking his balls and leering at them with the eyes of a billy-goat on heat, has not touched a hair of anyone's head, or even said an improper word.

"What videocassette?" asks the lady of the house, apparently determined to bluff things out and determinedly not looking at Quasimodo.

"The one related to the Jones murder," I say,

136

looking straight into her eyes, as is required in cases like these. She is still calm, too calm. She must have taken sedatives. She must have done, because no one can be that calm with Quasimodo around. She's putting on this show because she doesn't want to admit she's scared.

"As I already told you, I don't know anything about that."

"Jones filmed sadistic pornography. He organized orgies and blackmailed naive senators who somehow thought that getting a gorilla up their arse would cost them nothing."

She flushes. I am gratified to see that for the first time I have succeeded in imprinting anger on her stupid porcelain face.

"You're a very coarse person, and I hope never to have to see you again," she says faintly.

"I couldn't give a damn. What I want is the cassette."

"I found one, in a hidden space in a desk drawer. Perhaps that's what you're looking for, because it's disgusting."

"Where is it?"

"I'll bring it for you."

She stands up and goes upstairs to her bedroom. I'm frozen in my tracks. On the verge of victory, dumbfounded at the possibilities, each of which forks in front of me, offering different, even opposing, outcomes. Have I solved the case? Will I get to know who is behind the crimes? Will I get my hands on an object worth lots of money or blood? Will it be my turn to bet on all or nothing now: money forever, or six feet underground? One thing is certain: Carlos Hernandez will rise to whatever occasion might present itself.

Like a mechanical automaton in a house of horror, my colleague is still licking his disgusting chops, squinting to suggest his idea of a deranged assassin and continually pawing his bulging trouser-front. Seeing that the widow is no longer present to enjoy the show, he is dedicating his talents to the maid from Oaxaca, who every ten seconds or so comes to the kitchen door and stares at him in terror.

"That's enough, Quasimodo," I tell him. "You can stop now."

He puts his tongue away, folds his arms and adopts the stern expression of a public official.

"Aren't we going on with it?"

"There's no need. We've got what we wanted."

When the widow comes back down, the maid brings the coffee and pours it for us, taking great care to stay as far away as possible from Quasimodo.

"This is it," Estela says in a neutral tone. She hands me a black oblong which for a split second reminds me of the black spot – the sign of having been condemned to death – that the wooden-legged pirate gives Long John Silver in *Treasure Island*. In itself it's nothing: a videocassette. But premonitions of the future glitter in the dark plastic surface the size of my hand.

"Take it and leave," she goes on, in that tone of voice I find so pleasant whenever a suspect gives me orders.

I take the cassette and stand up. I gently squeeze her cheek between my thumb and forefinger. She tilts her head back, so I squeeze harder. It hurts. It humiliates her. I want to hurt and humiliate her. I want to hand her over to Quasimodo so he can rape and flog her all night, while I film him at it. No, that's not true. What I really want is to punish and rape her myself. I want to see her sobbing and begging me to stop, and I'll only forgive her when her misery and surrender are complete. She utters a short yelp, and her eyes brim with tears. I must look the picture of hatred, because the maid starts bawling too. Estela Lopez de Jones calls me an animal, a brute, a murderer and promises she'll get me thrown out of the police. "Shut up," I tell her. "When you're quiet, we'll talk." Quasimodo advances towards the maid, a finger on his mouth commanding silence. Immediate success: about to pass out, the maid turns white and becomes a statue. The widow is quiet too, sobbing gently. Her cheek really hurts. It will do for several days. At least I hope so. After I let go, she raises a hand to the white spot. Then she collapses into an armchair and goes on crying.

"We're going to watch the film here," I say. "All four of us. Where's the video?"

" . . . "

"I asked you where the video was."

139

Estela chokes back her tears, pouts. I put one finger under her chin and can feel her quiver.

"Upstairs. In the bedroom."

"Let's go, then."

A few minutes later it's all organized. Married life with Lourdes has led me to become an expert in unstable women. You need strength and patience in equal measure to create an atmosphere in which the woman no longer questions who's boss, and realizes the benefit of staying calm in order to prevent things getting even worse. Soon we're all installed in the bedroom. Quasimodo and me on the bed, Estela in a chair, and the maid sitting on the floor. The welcoming, plump, round altar presides over the scene. The film begins.

Snow White looks eighteen going on fifteen, with her short skirt and plaits, breasts like apples and 110 pounds of a mixture of innocence and sensuality all wrapped in tissue paper. There are only four, not seven dwarfs, and they are not real dwarfs, just very short men. Half-hidden behind false white beards, their faces are vicious and disturbing. The opening scene shows them having a meal in a clearing in a wood. One of the dwarfs is serving wine. He offers it to Snow White but switches the bottle without her realizing it. The four freaks wink and make obscene gestures to one another. They watch lasciviously as the woman-child sips from her glass. As she finishes her drink, Snow White falls into what appears to be a catatonic trance. The dwarfs pull a mattress out from under the table. They lay Snow White down on it and start to undress her. For three minutes, they fondle her avidly. Then they go to work with their mouths. One fastens onto a breast; Two sucks the other one; Three goes down between her legs. Bewildered, Snow White enjoys it. Four puts his prick in her mouth; she starts to suck. Four more minutes. The dwarfs strip off. They all have enormous pricks. In every imaginable position, sometimes one by one, at others all together, they fuck Snow White in the vagina, arse and mouth, performing their gymnastics for a further fifteen minutes. Two cops appear. The dwarfs run off naked into the wood. Snow White lifts a feeble hand. "Help me," she cries then screams.

*

All of a sudden no one is paying attention to the film any more. This is because a thin, fair-haired man has come into the room, gun in hand. He smiles unpleasantly. The widow mirrors his unpleasant smile. The rest of us look serious. Very serious.

"Are these the ones?" Blondie asks, as though there could be any doubt.

Estela Lopez de Jones nods. Then she slaps me as hard as she can. I can see her forcing herself to hide how much it hurts her hand.

I don't know why or how, but the next thing I know is Quasimodo and I are in a van, handcuffed and with handkerchiefs gagging our mouths, although this would not stop me speaking or shouting if I felt like it. But I don't because I couldn't care less. Also because of how deserted and dark the dirt road outside we're bumping our way along is. I wink at Quasimodo, and he winks back, twisting his snout in a smile under the gag to show he forgives me. I nod gratefully. If we get out of this alive, I'll install him in San Pedro de Los Pinos. He'll be my brother, and I'll use him to scare Lourdes whenever she tries to make me a slave to her outrageous whims.

The van comes to a halt. Estela and the maid haul us out roughly. I consider breaking their legs with a couple of well-aimed kicks, but there isn't time. "Two cops found dead on a back road." I'm the first. I collapse on the ground. I have a burning sensation everywhere except for my frozen chest. We're only given a fraction of a second to understand death.

"I don't like the look of this. He's got a fever." Miss Mengele put a hand on my brow; in the other she was wielding a syringe. Hernandez was nothing but shame and joy. Lots of shame and even more joy.

Chapter nineteen

So I got out of the clinic after spending three days there more or less in a coma, diagnosed as having cerebral concussion from severe trauma as a result of the accidental collision between my head and a stone, possibly during my rapid descent of the gully after having been shot at on a side-road on the way to Hidalgo.

I felt strange. Very strange. I couldn't understand what had made me behave the way I did against my boss, given the obvious fact that his is the hand that feeds me, the length of time I have been in the force, my career, my two families and the amount of money I need for their upkeep.

Nobody in their right mind would have done what I did. The only explanation must have been a temporary loss of my reasoning faculty due to concussion.

This was how I understood what had happened; but something inside me refused to accept it. I was assailed by grave disturbing thoughts that I had been on the verge of something tremendous, coded messages which suggested perhaps it had been the most important moment of my entire life, something intimately connected with the being or nothingness of Carlos Hernandez. A very romantic way of looking at it. Dreams of freedom that can't buy you a thing anywhere and that usually only serve to destroy the person deluded by them.

Something to remember, all the same.

My case might be a maze of complications, but it had more positive aspects too. The Commander had two choices: either he accepted that Carlos Hernandez was a traitor, a common delinquent who broke into his house and threatened him with a gun – and if he did this, that led to another choice, because he then either arrested Hernandez and faced the hazards of a trial, possibly revealing the laxness of his command, which other zealous defenders of law and order would be bound to point out, in the spirit of solidarity so characteristic of our police force. If he chose to do this, it could mean the end of his career, retirement and a future of playing dominoes or sitting outside his front door with a cigar in his mouth staring at women passers-by. If, on the other hand, he decided to liquidate the traitor, he would still have the problem of what to do with Quasimodo and Arganaraz. A difficult choice, because even he can't go around rubbing out everyone. Then again, he could decide to adopt the old adage of "nothing happened here". Or rather, something did happen – and not just anything, especially not something Hernandez is going to get off with lightly – but something that despite its serious nature can be controlled, particularly as far as the future is concerned. In other words: Hernandez suffered a temporary fit of madness, a mental overload due to the pressure of work, the sort of unhappy episode that can happen to anyone and lead them to commit outrages they themselves would find it hard to imagine in their normal state. On the basis of this diagnosis, there was hope that Hernandez might recover, as long as a strict and careful watch was kept on every stage of his progress. And despite the fact that this option meant leaving the dangerous individual – i.e. me – at large, it did seem to be the most convenient, least troublesome choice. I suppose my boss consulted someone, and in some elegant office or other one of our honourable citizens told him that if he could guarantee I was kept under control for the moment it would be better not to stir things up, because the main thing was to make sure the Jones case was well and truly closed.

In order to sound me out, the Commander asked me to dinner. I had spent three days eating boiled chicken in the clinic and with a treatment that kept me asleep the whole time, while elsewhere it was being decided whether it would be better to put me to sleep forever, so the sight of a plate of ravioli and a couple of bottles of Chianti seemed so attractive that I even felt capable of putting up with the Commander's pathetic attempts to recruit me again. Above all, I wanted to get out of there. In my delirium in the clinic I thought I had seen Lourdes and my kids. I knew I had tried to take on Estela Lopez de Jones, and had ended up as another victim of the blond assassin. I wanted to get out into the streets, to find Arganaraz and put a bullet in both his knees – although it was Quasimodo's deserting me that hurt most. I needed to see him to find out why he had thrown me to the wolves. I could imagine his excuses: "You looked so bad, Carlitos, that I thought I had to protect you, even against yourself."

The Commander greeted me as though nothing had happened and took twenty minutes to deliver his well-rehearsed speech. It went along the following lines: hierarchy – he was my boss and I was his subordinate; position – his was correct, I was mistaken; blackmail – in spite of all the extraordinary consideration he had shown me, not only had I been insubordinate, but I had committed offences which would cost me dear. If my attacks on the institution of the Mexican police ever got out, some people would be calling for my head on a plate. He himself was worried and hurt by what I had done, but also considered that only a severe mental disturbance, which had robbed me of my powers of reasoning, could explain my conduct; the bribe – considering all of which, as far as he personally was concerned and without being able to speak for others (others who were more dangerous, more vengeful than him), it was not entirely impossible for him to be able to understand – to forgive, he meant: he left the word itself floating in the air – and pretend that nothing had happened; then the offer to take me back: to which end he needed to know what I thought of my actions, and what my plans for the future were.

He was throwing me a lifeline. I needed one, but I was also mightily angry and wanted to settle the score with the paid assassin who had betrayed me. So that while I admitted he was right about everything and thanked him for being so patient – truly like a father, because only a father responds to attacks by not cutting off all links, whereas a friend would tell you to go to hell, refuse to talk to you and, if he were violent, smash your teeth in; a father on the other hand maintains the family bond and twists it round your neck so that you feel like a piece of shit for the rest of your life; regretted my evil actions, my only excuse being that being deranged is like being possessed by the Devil, forgetting who you are and what you really feel; accepted all the blame and said I was determined to spend the rest of my life making good the damage I had caused . . . I also regretted, well and truly regretted, that the responsibility was not being shared by the man who was the vilest person I had ever had the misfortune to meet.

"I'm talking about a sly double-crossing individual who is unworthy of wearing a policeman's uniform, a man as treacherous and poisonous as a snake. I'm talking about the coward who disarmed me at your house, simply to look good in your eyes, when he was the one who took advantage of my bout of madness to incite me to commit those criminal acts, which I am still at a loss to explain how I came to agree to."

147

I was sending him to jail. Why not? Arganaraz was a bastard who had ruined the most important thing Hernandez had done in years: to create that look of terror in the purple face of this other bastard who was buying me with Chianti.

The Commander turned to the question of my companions. It was shameful. We had formed a gang, and that could damage the reputation of our Mexican institutions. What was he to do with us?

It was obvious he was trying to get information and to win me over. Fifty-fifty. I'll forgive you, if you can guarantee there'll be no problems. Come up with solutions, because you're the one in trouble. I can and will help you, but I'm not going to take any risks. Got it?

Yes, sir.

"Quasimodo is my friend, and I'll vouch for him," I said. The monster was going to owe me another favour, and this time he'd be paying me back for a long, long time. "He was as confused as I was – all he really wanted to do was to help. He must feel remorse for what we did and will be grateful if you show him mercy. And given the amount of information he can lay his hands on, having him grateful could be no bad thing for any future collaboration that might improve the DO's performance.

"But I'm worried about Arganaraz as well," I said.

The Commander poured more Chianti, which meant now we were plotting about how to get me back on the force. I helped him find a practical and even-handed solution. There was no way he could pardon three loose cannons who had not played by the rules. That would be to undermine his authority. But if he pardoned two and punished one, his authority and fairness would not be called into question. On the contrary, he would be praised for being both decisive and understanding. I suggested he send Arganaraz to Chiapas, Oaxaca or Sinaloa. Let's see how he got on with the Indians and drug traffickers. I had been thinking of leaving him crippled for life, but the ravioli and Chianti put me in a generous mood, making me feel tolerant and forgiving.

I left the restaurant a pardoned man, a member of the DO once again.

Chapter twenty

The office I work in is like a microcosm. I usually get thoughts like that when I return to it after several days away and find that nobody seems to have done a thing apart from stuff themselves with sandwiches and use sensitive files to wrap them in. The wastepaper baskets are full of condoms that have apparently been put to good use. The few people who have decided to catch up a bit on their work have created even more of a mess: waiting on my desk for me is a huge pile of papers, which only the prevailing stupidity of Mexican bureaucracy could see as being of any interest whatsoever.

Silver Bullet was not in yet. I growled at the secretaries from afar and climbed into my cage to make a call.

Quasimodo sounded genuinely pleased to hear me. He had some news. The Lizard's gang had been caught: the delinquents who for weeks had been terrorizing the residential neighbourhood of Copilco with their break-ins. More than ten houses had been burgled when no one was at home; in other cases, the owners and their servants had been mistreated and abused. Quasimodo and I had talked about it before, and now he was offering the information in case it might be of some use to me. The Lizard and his gang were perfect collaborators: they accused each other so extensively that the police had completely wrapped up the case already, and the public prosecutor, seeing that there were no extenuating circumstances, would be calling for two hundred years in prison. Estela Lopez de Jones's house was not mentioned in any of their statements, which was understandable because it was merely an attempted break-in, besides which no one can expect the criminal to do the detective work on the police's behalf.

Maribel is a transparent woman. Even without being able to hear what she was saying, just by watching her from ten yards away anyone can tell that the boss is not in the office and at the far end of the line there's some poor guy trying to control his hard-on.

*

"This is getting worse all the time," the Commander had said, pointing at me with his glass of Chianti. "We're faced with a poisonous, red-hot affair, one of those you end up getting burned by if you're not careful. Look: we've got a gringo, a Cuban and two Colombians murdered. That means three embassies are involved. Listen closely. Apparently, the gringo was a high-flyer, because as soon as the US Embassy gets involved, everything becomes very hush-hush. The Cuban was a typical anti-Castro nut, with a criminal record that would get him thrown out of a sewer. And he's murdered right now, just when relations between Mexico and Cuba are full of too many imponderables for those of us caught in the middle. And we never know what Colombians are really up to, even though everyone knows that to say 'Colombia' is to say drugs. Sometimes I think the right of asylum and all that is a good idea. But unfortunately, times have changed. In Lazaro Cardenas's day, it was the children of Morelia and boatloads of Spanish poets who arrived. Now we get Marielitos and drug traffickers; Uruguayans who've taken over the sale of encyclopaedias; Argentinians who are pushing Mexicans out of all the university posts; starving Guatemalans and Salvadorians who don't even know how to sell books door-to-door and don't have a single university graduate among them even if you pay to find one; and that's not counting the Chileans, who are like air pollution because they get in everywhere. You know me. I hate racism. But we Mexicans are big-hearted, and our generosity isn't always repaid as it should be. Look how we were expelled from international football for two years. The Guatemalans flood our frontiers with fleeing criminals and think that's fine, but if one of ours makes a mistake writing his birth date they want to take us to the United Nations. Give me a break! But to return to what we were talking about: it's a mess. It has to be dealt with, Officer."

While the Commander was saying all this, I took advantage to forge ahead with the ravioli and

152

wine. "It's time to organize another party with those girls of yours," he said, and I ate another mouthful. "I've got another bundle of dollars and I need a buyer," and I knocked back more wine. "Either we look after ourselves or we'll lose money, Hernandez," he went on, while I made a start on the dessert and realized that he wasn't going to send me to the cemetery because he needed someone to take on all these tasks for him. When he paused for breath, I asked:

"What are we going to do, boss?"

That wasn't an easy question, and there would be no easy answer. The proof of which was that there was no answer at all from him.

"You're in charge of the case."

"And you give the orders."

He smiled. The way someone on the make smiles at someone else on the make, when they don't get in each other's way.

"As long as we don't have sufficient reason to change our point of view, we'll have to continue with our first line of enquiry. But after carrying out your investigation and information-gathering, and bearing in mind the relevant considerations, tell me whether you have any specific ideas which might bring positive results, without affecting any outside interests and respecting all the different possible jurisdictions."

Typical DO shit.

He paused again then roared:

"We've got to put a stop to this Godawful mess once and for all!"

Time to show I could be precise and efficient.

"Yes. I've got an idea, boss," I told him.

The Commander's smile broadened.

"I wasn't making an idle comment, Officer, but simply seeking to remove all doubt as to who was my best man. Tell me your idea."

I told him.

*

Silver Bullet came into the office, saw me and went off to talk to Laura. I realized he was upset with me because he felt Quasimodo had taken his place. And since to be a boss means making concessions, balancing the general good with one's own, not to mention the little matter of a backlog of payments I needed the help of an assistant to collect, I called him over and – after explaining in minute detail what I would do to him if he even thought of trying to pull a fast one or in any way of going beyond the mission I was entrusting him with – I sent him off to meet Rosario, collect my debt and arrange an appointment in two days' time.

I immediately saw it was a mistake: his eyes shone far too brightly.

After I left the office I phoned Jones's widow. She was thinking of travelling to Colombia in four days. I told her what her trip depended on.

*

The Lizard was called Rodolfo Angel Osorio Mena. He was twenty-four, lank, dyed-blond hair, a

154

shiny black eye and a huge split mouth which gave him his nickname. He was wearing black trainers, black jeans and T-shirt with a red design on it. He stood in a corner of the cell and stared at me suspiciously.

"I've said all I'm going to say. I want to see my lawyer," he shouted, suddenly full of concern about the law.

"I'm your lawyer, Lizard," I told him. "I've come for a little chat."

"What about?"

"I've got a proposal for you."

"I don't talk to the filth." The Lizard was one big frown, a cinematographic diabolical rock star who had declared all-out war on the order a heartless society had imposed.

I gave a loud belly laugh. I know lots of pieces of shit like him. Kids who are worthless, who won't work or follow a timetable or have any sense of duty or feel the slightest responsibility for anyone else. They all end up off their heads, sniffing glue and stabbing their best friend to get their hands on a few pesos. I'm a father, and I have no time for them; I only have to think of my daughter and I want to give them a good kicking.

"Suit yourself, Lizard," I said, still chuckling. "If you don't like my proposal, I'm out of here, you'll never see me again, and you're done for. You're the one in trouble, and it's up to you whether you want to be smart or stupid."

"What do you want from me?" he growled.

I stared at him for several moments, applying

the "Hernandez Method", guaranteed to make anyone nervous.

"Look, Lizard," I said, very coolly and calmly. "What with the crimes you and your friends have confessed to, plus any unresolved case some cop or other in Copilco decides to pin on you, you're looking at thirty to forty years in prison. Let's say it's thirty and that with good conduct you only have to spend twenty years inside. By the time you get out, you'll be forty-four years old. You'll be a walking ruin, with all your youth spent behind bars. Are you married?"

". . ."

"I'm asking you whether you're married."

"Yes."

"What's going to happen to you wife in those twenty years?"

". . ."

"You're right, it doesn't bear thinking about. We both know perfectly well what she can expect, husbandless for twenty years . . . If you want to lie to yourself, you can tell yourself every day that it's not your fault. You can tell that to the rapists and murderers you meet in the prison recreation yard. Do you have any children . . . ?"

". . ."

"Not very talkative, are you?"

"Just one, he's two years old."

"Congratulations. In five or six years perhaps you'll be able to decorate your cell with a photo of him working as a clown at a set of traffic lights."

The Lizard clenched his fists, restraining himself from launching himself at me and strangling me. I'd have liked him to try. I haven't been keeping up with my classes of boxing and karate so it would be good to get some of the rust off by using my hands and feet on a real opponent. But the Lizard was very weak, and his future looked grim enough without adding to it the charge of assaulting a police officer. So he gradually cooled down. Still full of loathing, he was tempted by curiosity and a glimmer of hope. He spat at me:

"Stop playing games! Finish with this shit and tell me what you want!"

"Fine. This is my offer: you get off scot-free in a case of legitimate self-defence. You'll be kept in remand while your case is being heard, and after that you're a free man. We guarantee it won't take more than a year and, of course, the verdict will be in your favour."

No suspects trust the police, and it's not for me to say whether they're right or not. I wasn't expecting him to be any different. I went on:

"I'll swap all the charges against you, which include two rapes and an attempted murder, as well as a whole string of break-ins, GBHs and damage to property and so on, for a single one which with a few technical adjustments we could call self-defence."

"Aha, so you're the cop from Copilco with an unresolved case he wants to pin on someone," the Lizard said with a couple of ironic grins.

"Could be," I said. "But to you it's worth it. And if it suits both of us, why not take advantage of it?"

"I need all the information." The Lizard was beginning to feel like a crocodile. "And I still want to talk to my lawyer."

"Who is your lawyer?"

"My wife is the one who talks to him. So I'll have to tell her, and to do that, you'll have to let me out of solitary."

I'm a cop. I breakfast on bravado and lunch on psychological pressure. I handed him a pen and paper.

"Write down your lawyer's name. I promise I'll bring him here. You'll get out of solitary just as soon as we make a deal. Does your wife live at the address you gave?"

"Yes. They've already been and wrecked my apartment. You'd better ask – my wife may have been arrested too, and that'll save you a journey."

"Don't get cute, Lizard. What's your wife's name?"

"Roxana Erika Ibarra."

*

As I thought, for a female of the species to be adorned with names like that, she couldn't be more than twenty. Roxana Erika was tall and slim, with a beautiful but vulgar face to which a slight cast in one eye added a strange touch. She lived in an apartment in Colonia Doctores which seemed to be overflowing with objects, as the police had strewn everything all over the place in their search.

I had a word with the cop on guard and shut myself in a bedroom to talk to Roxana.

Roxana Erika was a typical neighbourhood girl whose mind had been fed by TV and women's magazines. She had been cast onto the stormy seas of life with few skills to help her. She looked scared, but pleased at the friendly way I introduced myself – very different from that of the other cops who had barked orders at her and even fondled her, completely disrespectful of little Osman Israel asleep in his cot.

Knowing the mother's name, the baby's didn't take me by surprise. I got straight to the point, and a little while later myself, Roxana and Doctor Cuauhtemoc Nava Ordaz were sitting in the dark and dusty hole the lawyer called an office on Calle Venezuela.

I had scarcely opened my mouth before the lawyer demanded guarantees for his client. That gave me the chance to ask if he were new in his profession, and if by chance he knew of anything more flexible than the word of a policeman.

"I want to put an end to this business today," I told him. "Come with me, and we'll settle the charge sheet in an hour."

We had no time to take Roxana home, so we left her at a cinema and I promised to return in two hours and tell her how things had gone. I drew the lawyer an outline of the situation. We'd put all the robberies in Copilco onto the Lizard's accomplices. We'd get rid of any statements that might incriminate him as ringleader. To keep the others happy we'd offer them mitigating circumstances and a lower sentence. If they didn't like the idea (which was hard to imagine), we'd keep interrogating them until they softened up. Luckily, Nava Ordaz was to act as lawyer for all of them, and was happy to do all he could to reach a quick and satisfactory solution. The Lizard would be the man who went into the hotel with Jones. (His dyed yellow hair was useful for something). Jones assaulted him, and the Lizard killed him defending himself. We would invent links between the two men. Jones's wife would swear she knew him. For reasons that belonged to the secret nature of the investigation – reasons linked to the widow's future, to her idea of returning to Colombia in three days, to the scandal she could find herself in ... in a word, for reasons that had to do with enjoying life with lots of money versus a penniless destiny. It was an easy choice, which I knew had already been made, so I was in a position to assure the lawyer that everything would go smoothly. We would say the Lizard had been Jones's chauffeur and bodyguard. In the hotel, the pair of them would be pretty drunk, they would argue, Jones would pull out a gun, there would be a struggle, then the fatal shot. Finish, kaput, see you later, alligator.

"What about the blonde woman who went into the hotel with Jones?"

"Concentrate on the blond guy who came out. I'll talk to the owner and the manager of the hotel. A hotel of that sort exists in a legal limbo, and the only guarantee for it to stay open is to be on good terms with the police. I'm sure the manager won't remember too much about a person who 'stayed in the shadows'."

I was waiting for the inevitable comment. I wasn't wrong.

"All this is . . . how shall I put it . . . a little extraordinary, Officer. Or at least, shall we say, unusual. Of course, we're all here to help the forces of law and order in any way we can, but we have to tie up certain loose ends . . . "

The lawyer's drivel was nauseating. I let him finish.

"Just imagine the difficulty of my position! The unexpected problems that could affect my career! I'm not sure I could take this on for my usual fees."

"There's a middleman."

"What do you mean?"

"A fence who bought all the things the Lizard and his gang stole."

"So?"

"My colleagues who were first on the spot took various things as evidence. Fortunately, I have managed to make some arrangements, which you don't need to know the details of, but which in short mean that this man will go free. As from tomorrow, you and I will make sure he pays us his taxes, which we will share out in democratic proportions."

"How democratic?"

"Don't be in such a hurry, Your Honour. You'll get your cut."

*

Two hours later, feeling sweaty, exhausted and bittersweet, I signed off and shut the files that I had been drawing up under Nava Ordaz's close scrutiny.

I could feel forty pounds of stress weighing on the back of my neck, screaming for me to have a lengthy shower and a session with any of the Three Marias. One of those when you lie there quite still, watching, while the girl does all the work.

In my hands I had a nicely tied up piece of work; in my mouth I had the taste of a rat that lasted a full week. Too bad. That's the game, and if you want to play it, sometimes you have to clean the toilets. Too big, too many interests for Carlos Hernandez to try to take on windmills. Of course it shouldn't be like that, of course the world is a mess. Nothing new there. Reality is like a low-life bar: you have to be drunk to feel good in it. I'm on the side of change; that's why I vote Cardenas. Some day we'll win, and then . . .

I called the Commander and told him the good news. I made a few vague comments for the sake of the phone spirits and arranged to meet him the next day in the Diplomatico to sort out the details. The Commander was having breakfast with an important official at nine, so he told me to come at half past eight, the asshole!

I picked up Roxana Erika and took her home. I

spared her the intricate details that might have confused her little mind, emphasized the benefits for the Lizard, and told her the case had been resolved satisfactorily and that we would give her economic support, thanks to a thrifty intermediary. I saw no need to tell her that it was the Lizard who had insisted on this help for her.

Roxana Erika started to look at me as if I were the Lone Ranger, and by one of those strange coincidences life sometimes grants us, I also felt an immediate sympathy for her.

I could still feel the pressure on the back of my neck. I looked across at the harmonious angles of Roxana's silhouette, and regretted all that beauty was wasted on marriage to the Lizard. I was soon imagining her going cross-eyed during an orgasm and, almost without noticing it, my hand strayed to her warm knee.

She jumped in her seat, gave me a furious cross-eyed glare and pressed herself again the car door, leaving me with my arm dangling and looking completely ridiculous.

I muttered an apology, and we continued on our way in silence. I was thinking that human beings' reliance on routine would, with time, change her way of looking at me. When I turned up at her apartment on the first of each month bearing an envelope stuffed with money and a doll for her little monster Osman Israel, Roxana Erika would get used to expecting me, perhaps with a touch of anxiety. Then we'd see.

We picked the boy up from a neighbour's

apartment. A woman in housecoat and hair in rollers, who stared at me the whole time with obvious disapproval, putting into her sour stare all the distaste she and her kind feel for forty-year-old cops who invade other people's homes.

When I left them, my neck was still throbbing.

Chapter twenty-one

Lourdes came back. I know because Gloria hangs up as soon as she hears my voice, and if my children answer the phone they say "Leave a message, sir; my mother will call you back as soon as she can." I know because my breakfast beer is either warm or freezing again. I know because my things appear to move around the house with a mind of their own, and I can never find them where I left them, and because my pockets look as though someone's gone through them, and my notebooks seem to have been read over. I know because Carlos and Araceli, who, thanks to the warmth of my paternal influence, behaved impeccably while their mother was taking her vacation, are now once again filling the house with rock'n'roll layabouts, stoned schizophrenics and other wonderful specimens of modern Mexico.

Lourdes came back. This is the second time, and, according to her, there can never be a third. I really admire this woman. I admire the amazing capacity she has to turn any situation that affects both of us into a triumph on her part. I'm fascinated by the way she has of coming back as though she were a queen who, thanks to an over-generous heart, allows herself the luxury of pardoning the faithless governor of her colonies, despite all the evidence of his heinous crimes. If it were me returning, Lourdes would see to it that I was forced to do so with my head down and my tail between my legs. A repentant and pleading beggar, who she would listen to with the appropriate mistrust and condescension and would forgive little by little, making sure he was first put through repeated scenes of humiliation. The same situation changes its meaning and content radically depending on which of us is the protagonist. Lourdes – who had not been able to prepare so much as a sandwich for her children before casting them into oblivion – comes back and everything is hunky-dory. I have simply to roll out the red carpet, attend to her every desire and modify my bad habits and disorderly way of life, which apparently are the causes threatening our family harmony.

I considered buying my wife the carpet-cleaner I'd been promising her for years and put a few ice cubes in my beer to finish it off. As Lourdes came and went in the bedrooms, she treated me to a magical glimpse of her body, which gave me an urgent desire to make love to her. I realized she was employing the full range of her talents, and the thought pleased me, because if there's no more sense of adventure between a man and a woman, the whole thing's had it.

I called the office, and everything was under control. Silver Bullet had not arrived, the Commander was having breakfast, and Maribel used her best airport announcement voice. My tasks for the day consisted of placing forty thousand greenbacks, first-class Colombian in origin, welcome even on Wall Street, and controlling my dolt of an assistant, who was paying a little more attention than I needed to the Three Marias.

Our kids were at school. Just time for a quick session with Lourdes before my shower. Who knows, in ten years from now I might not be able to.

Chapter twenty-two

Her little apple breasts and body lubricated by all the sexual activity, Victoria Ledesma looks eighteen going on fifteen. When the cops appear, the dwarfs run off naked into the wood. Victoria raises a hand to ask for help then screams with pain as one of the cops beats her with his stick. She is thrown face down on the mattress and the stick is forced up her. Afterwards, one of the cops pulls out an enormous knife. Victoria Ledesma does not see the flash of light rising, falling, then rising again, dripping blood.

**BITTER LEMON PRESS
LONDON**

Bringing you the best literary crime and *romans noirs* from Europe, Africa and Latin America.

Thumbprint   *Friedrich Glauser*

A classic of European crime writing. Glauser, the Swiss Simenon, introduces Sergeant Studer, the hero of five novels.

January 2004   ISBN 1–904738–00–1   £8.99 pb

Holy Smoke   *Tonino Benacquista*

A story of wine, miracles, the mafia and the Vatican. Darkly comic writing by a best-selling author.

January 2004   ISBN 1–904738–01–X   £8.99 pb

The Russian Passenger   *Günter Ohnemus*

An offbeat crime story involving the Russian mafia but also a novel of desperate love and insight into the cruel history that binds Russia and Germany.

March 2004   ISBN 1–904738–02–8   £9.99 pb

Tequila Blue   *Rolo Diez*

A police detective with a wife, a mistress and a string of whores. This being Mexico, he resorts to arms dealing, extortion and money laundering to finance the pursuit of justice.

May 2004   ISBN 1–904738–04–4   £8.99 pb

Goat Song   *Chantal Pelletier*

A double murder at the Moulin Rouge. Dealers, crack addicts and girls dreaming of glory who end up in porn videos.

July 2004   ISBN 1–904738–03–6   £8.99 pb

The Snowman   *Jörg Fauser*

Found: two kilos of Peruvian flake, the best cocaine in the world. Money for nothing. A fast-paced crime novel set in Malta, Munich and Ostend.

September 2004   ISBN 1–904738–05–2   £8.99 pb

www.bitterlemonpress.com